Struggle and Chaos in three Countries

RENATA PLITZKO

Struggle and Chaos in three Countries

Based on a true story
Available in English an German

The names and other identifying characteristics of the persons included in this memoir have been changed.

Bibliographical Information of the Deutsche Nationalbibliothek
This publication is listed in the Deutsche Nationalbibliographie of the Deutsche Nationalbibliothek; detailed bibliographical information can be accessed under http: //dnb.d-nb.de

Printing, Production and Layout: BoD – Books on Demand, Norderstedt
ISBN: 978-3-7357-6472-0

This Book is dedicated:

IN LOVING MEMORY OF MY GRANDMOTHER
Emilia Krawcyk
(1908 – 1968)

You will forever be with me in thought and spirit.
I wish you were here.

ACKNOWLEDGMENTS

I am grateful to my friends for their valuable time and energy in helping to transcribe and edit this book, making it into a wonderful instrument for dialogue.

Table of contents

PROLOGUE

I peered out my window, looking down from thirty-three thousand feet. A placid, azure blue sky surrounded me for now. To be sure, there had been turbulence before, and there would likely be turbulence again. But for now, it was calm and I had long since learned to weather a storm. It is autumn, 2012 and I'm planning an expedition – a pilgrimage of sorts. Traveling to my place of birth to visit the family I left behind so far away, I yearn to re-trace my roots.

Far below, ghostly clouds pass indifferently, as indifferently as the mists of time have passed by me. As we near our destination, I close my eyes and remember that day years ago, and the younger woman who left under such different circumstances.

The younger woman left with nothing. My older version returns as a self-made woman. I left as a German and returned as a German-American. We left at a moment's notice, those years long ago. Only two weeks before I left the first time, I could never have foreseen any reason to hotfoot it to Switzerland, nor any necessity to immigrate to the United States. Yet, for all my changes in fortune now I am, in many ways, the same person who took that leap of faith years ago – a survivor, a maker, a *take-it-as-it-comes* kind of woman.

The plane began its descent to Frankfurt International Airport. Today, it is a beautiful, crisp autumn day, in stark contrast to the nightmarish flight from Zurich to New York in the winter of 1982. There is no fear like the fear of the unknown, but on that day in 1982, I remained convinced that whatever lay ahead must surely beat the alternative – what could have been, had I chosen to remain in Germany. All I could do at that time was to put my best foot forward.

PART ONE

CHAPTER ONE

THE NEW WORLD

That day, as I sat miles above the frigid sea, contemplating what future the New World held, the pilot's voice came over the intercom in a stereotypically, indifferent monotone.

"Two hours out from JFK International Airport," he said, halting to clear his throat. "It looks like we might be in for some rough weather. I'll keep you posted on the details as we make our approach, in the meantime relax and thanks for flying air..."

I did not understand English, and Frank sat two rows away. Because the tickets were booked last-minute, the airline could not arrange for us to be seated together. My neighboring passenger, an elderly white-bearded man, kindly explained that it would be snowing in New York.

A short time later, the *fasten seatbelt* light came on. Soon after, the carry-on luggage began to shake and rattle in the overhead storage. The plane shuddered, as if hitting potholes in the sky. The older gentleman told me, almost as if to reassure himself, that no plane had ever crashed as a result of turbulence.

An hour passed by, in nerve-racking manner, before the pilot relayed a breaking weather report. Apparently, the plane was headed into no mere flurry, nor anything as inconsequential as a blizzard. The danger which awaited our arrival in New York was none other than a meteorological phenomenon unique to the eastern United States, a veritable frozen hurricane: a Nor'easter.

Heavy snow streaked through the air, driven by buffeting, shrieking winds. The airplane's wings shuddered in the swirling winds of the storm as the pilot navigated blinding conditions in the approach. Over the intercom, came more words indecipherable to me.

"The pilot is saying that he is a veteran of bad-weather flying, and that there is nothing to worry about," my neighbor reported.

But this admission, it seemed, only served to provide more tension to the already nervous passengers. *If the weather was not dangerous, the pilot would have no need to assure us of his abilities would he?* I began to wonder whether I had jumped out of the frying pan and into the fire on this trip.

The 747 touched down with a screech. The airbrakes were thrown on, and the plane came roaring to a halt. It landed without any complications. *Despite everything,* I contemplated, *despite the dangerous weather, despite the run-in with the police, despite the frenzied exodus, despite all the planes, trains, and automobiles, I had arrived in one piece – or had I?*

The plane came coasting to a stop. A tractor came alongside the plane, one of those awkward, square-ish variety, rumbling and smoking with diesel fumes.

In retrospect, I recall that the tractor's driver, who was bundled up like an Eskimo, seemed a little frenzied. Naturally, the ground crew of any airport are trained to hustle, and this would have been doubly true considering the raging storm. Yet, there was also an uneasiness in the tractor driver's movement, almost as if he was afraid of something, I sensed. He hitched the plane and headed down the strip.

It seemed like we were being towed for a long time. Some of the passengers grew uneasy. They began to mutter under their breath or whisper to their neighbors. The flight attendants moved to the front of the plane and talked among themselves behind a closed curtain. Then someone shouted something in English, in an angry voice. "We are being taken away from the terminal." It was true. We were.

Through the gusting curtain of snow, the passengers could see that the plane had been parked at a dead-end; a corner of the airport far away from the terminal. I watched, meanwhile, as the tractor took off with all the speed it could muster.

At any other time, this corner of the airport might have been a sight to behold, viewed safely out of the elements. The tempest screamed across the frost-bitten marshland upon which the airport was built. The grey waters of Jamaica Bay frothed and foamed. Across the bay, the lights of the New York City skyline could be seen, glimmering faintly. The view was bleak and yet somehow still beautiful, but any appreciation for natural beauty was lost on us passengers, in light of the anxiety we were now feeling.

After several seemingly unbearable minutes, an announcement drifted over the sound system. The captain's voice, filled with duress, explained to all aboard that we must, at all costs, remain calm. I did not need to see the fear on the faces around me, I did not need Frank to explain to me what was being said. I had heard the captain use a word that I understood full-well, and that understanding was enough to send me into a tailspin. That word was *bomb*. I found my life flashing before my eyes, as indeed, must have been the case with everyone else on board.

I had always been one to rise above circumstances. If that were not the case, I would never have set foot on the train to leave Germany; I would never have boarded the plane for America. But had I finally encountered an insurmountable obstacle? What escape could there be from this terrible predicament? What could I have done differently?

It was a cruel trick of destiny to have put me on that plane. Two weeks before, I had no plans to travel to America. Two weeks in the future, the journey would have been an impossibility – the airlines would not have allowed it. Why? Because I was seven-and-a-half months pregnant. Airlines, not to mention doctors, prohibit eight-month expectant mothers from flying. Yet here I sat, in a plane with a bomb about to go off.

CHAPTER TWO

GOING HOME

Returning to the present, the passengers beside me are calm and the weather is fair as the skyscrapers of Frankfurt come into view.

It is said that diamonds are made of pieces of coal, which are put under immense pressure. At first glance, no one would think that a piece of coal could make such a transformation. This same transformation can be compared to me, I suppose. I am similar to a piece of coal. I came from humble beginnings. I have endured tremendous pressure throughout my life, but I have never let it affect me negatively. It has simply made me stronger.

To understand the diamond and compare it to myself, I know I must think back to what a lump of coal goes through to transform it into a diamond. Where did it originally come from? What pressures of life did it undergo, and how did it keep itself from being crushed or burned up in the process? As I continue to revisit my origins – the place where I experienced the brunt of life's pressures – in my mind, I resolve that the only way to understand this process is for me to travel to my ancestral home in Poland.

I intended to visit the house that we left behind in 1966 with nothing. It is the house in which I was born. My mother was pregnant (with me) when the house was under construction. I cannot help but still feel incredulity at what I have managed to overcome since my birth.

My mother was helping to build the house. She was nine months pregnant and an extremely tough woman. As she worked, she felt the baby coming. "I need to stop," she said, "I am going to have the baby." My father called for a nurse, and my mother delivered me in the house. When I go to Poland, I will take a picture of the room where I was born.

It was a different time and a different place. My mother rested for a little while, then she simply got out of bed and continued to help my father to build the house. I marvel at her strength and fortitude.

I was born on September 27, 1956, the third child of Irma and Karl Plitzko. Later in life mother would reveal her marriage was, in the social sense, arranged. She had not wanted to marry my father, but with her parent's insistence she had reluctantly consented.

She was born in northern Poland in the town of Walcen, in the region of Oberschlesien. You may recall a country known as the Free State of Prussia. Poland and Germany were in contention for control over Prussia in both World Wars. In the aftermath of World War II, most of Prussia was absorbed by Germany. But the region of Oberschlesien, or in English, *Upper Silesia* was ceded to Poland.

In the years that followed, Russia reached an iron hand over Europe, building satellite offices throughout to report back certain activities. It was certainly an infiltration process to gain power throughout Europe. Poland, in particular, was the target of Soviet designs. After World War II, Russian leadership constituted a large part of both Polish government and military leadership. With Russian control everywhere, fear and malaise came to the people of Poland.

Living in Poland, we always had to be careful. Our radio at home could pick up German stations, but my parents were always afraid of playing them; there was a lot of paranoia among us all. It was for good reason, too. There were spies everywhere. I thought of them as soldiers in plain clothes. Now I realize they were some sort of secret police.

In preparation for the move, my mother taught us to speak German. One day, as we were having our lesson, I noticed a man listening at the window and told her about it. Of course, that horrified her. From that time on, we held our lessons in secret, behind closed doors.

It was not until the late 1950s that Poland successfully began to assert its independence. It was a period marked with general public unease and, in its wake, many Poles especially Oberschlesiens, absconded to West Germany.

I was very young then, too young to remember, but my impression was that we left for political reasons. At the time, many fled to Germany. We left in a train full of people – many in the same situation as we were. My parents gave our house away; they didn't even bother to sell it. All we took with us was a feather blanket. We had to leave everything else behind. It made me so sad.

The family relocated to the town of Kesselstadt, in Hessen, West Germany. Located only fifteen minutes from the bustling city of Frankfurt, Kesselstadt boasts a rich history. Notable residents include none other than the *Brothers Grimm* of fairy tale acclaim.

My father, already had a brother living in Germany. This, and the promise of work and a new start, gave him the confidence to relocate his young family. Then, as now, the Frankfurt metropolitan area was an economically-thriving area, with plenty of jobs ready for the taking. After a short stint in Friedland, our newly- naturalized German family was made welcome in Kesselstadt. There was no xenophobia, or resentment of immigrants in Kesselstadt. To the contrary we, who arrived with nothing, were provided for with housing made especially available to those just beginning to get on their feet in the new land. Simply to make things a little easier, my mother and father legally changed the spelling of our names to their German form.

Unfortunately, although our family left Poland to escape the turmoil of the Cold War, we also brought along with us a measure of chaos.

I did not have a good upbringing. My father was a drunk, and when he drank, he would beat us children. He was very violent. My father was one of those people (I hate to say) who was best left six feet under.

A powerful declaration, yet it is fact. I say this not in a tone of disdain, bitterness, or with any hatred, for that matter. I have, to a greater degree, moved past the pain my father brought me. It is forty years now since I moved out of my parent's house, but one can guess that emotional wounds such as mine might leave scars, ever-present in the shaping of how I see myself and the world. However, I truly believe that one's reaction to adversity is a choice we need to make. One has the ability to choose how to handle circumstances either negatively or positively.

My father could never hold down a job for long. Mother worked long hours at the local post office, from five-thirty in the morning until nine-thirty at night. Her absence at home left a vacuum of responsibility, most of which was filled by me, the middle child of a brood of five. Father's perpetual state of inebriation only served to compound the difficulties we children faced, with an often-absent mother.

One day, rather than going in to work at his current, short-lived job in manufacturing, father stayed home and chose to drink instead. A few hours into the work day, his boss phoned our house hoping to learn why he was absent.

I answered the phone. He asked to speak with my father. I told him that he was home and asked him to hold on. I was only a child at the time and I could see no reason to lie.

Despite his state of intoxication, father had overheard the conversation from the next room. In a fit of drunken rage, he confronted me, slamming the phone down in the process.

"Why did you tell him I am here?" He demanded. "You should have told him I am sick. You should have told him I was away." He then proceeded to beat me.

He kicked me in the back. I fell. I couldn't stand up on my own, so I stayed on the floor where I had fallen. It was not until hours later, with the aid of my mother who had just returned from work, that I was able to stand with help. After this event, I made it my life-policy never to lie for anyone.

Perhaps it is commonplace for older generations to recoil at the fashions of the youth of their day. Sadly, the ensuing backlash in this instance was anything but normal.

Another occasion in the Plitzko household served to typify my father's violent nature, meted out especially to me. In the 1960s, culture was changing, and we three oldest girls, Ava, Else, and I did not want to be left behind. One day, we found some nail polish. We were going out, so we put some on. It was only very lightly colored. But when my father saw us, he flew off the handle. He threatened us. "You are not going out like that!" he roared.

Then, he took a sharp knife and forced us all to scrape the polish off our fingernails.

I could never say anything or tell anyone about it; no one would believe me. Back then, there was no public outcry against child abuse. Child protective services were far less advanced and children didn't have the same rights as they do now.

It was a different time and a different culture. People would say that, *the father is in charge, the children have a duty to listen to their father and he has the right to do what he thinks is best.* Adding, *probably, he had good reason to hit you.* If I had told anyone at home, they would probably have asked, "What did you do Renata?" If I had told anyone at school, they would likely would not have believed me. I felt hopeless.

My mother suffered so about her husband's violent outbursts, but she also felt powerless to confront him. His alcoholism prevented any reasoning with him. Additionally, domestic abuse and addiction services were not widely known or available at the time.

There was no 800 number hotline to call in case of abuse; we were on our own. Today, if anyone tried to do half the things my father did, they would be jailed, and the key thrown away.

While she may have been powerless to prevent her husband's violent actions, my mother always expressed to us that she strongly disapproved of his actions, and assured us how much she regretted ever having submitted to the arranged marriage.

Fortunately, over the last half-century, society's views on child abuse have changed drastically. Domestic abuse is now viewed in a much more serious light. Protective services are widely known and utilized, and the legal system is slanted towards the welfare of the child. In some ways, as I would learn years later, the legal system has come around full-circle.

CHAPTER THREE

TRIALS AND TRIBULATIONS

At first glance, one would never guess the things I have lived through. I feel I am a physically unimposing woman with a conservative demeanor and my accent is rich with my native German tongue. But, anyone who interacts with me in person will see something of a fire in my eyes, and will detect conviction in my energy. Then one will know that my words *never give up, believe in yourself,* are more than just words. They come from a hard-gained wisdom; a way of life experienced in full. They are much more than a mere fortune-cookie mantra. They are words of hard-bought truth. Truths which I hope to pass on to anyone who will listen.

This is why I want to get my life on paper. I want to help people. Maybe if others are in the same circumstances, they will have hope. My hope is that they will say, *this Renata person made it, then so can I.* You have got to have faith. It cannot be overemphasized that my life is characterized by an absence of apathy. At a second glance, one might find this claim confusing. Apathy itself, one might say, is the absence of something – a lack of passion or purpose. Thus, one might argue, it could better be expressed by saying that my life is characterized by a passion and purpose. While this is true, it is not the whole truth.

Apathy is the most natural thing in the world. When people encounter obstacles that seem too big to handle, indifference is oftentimes the answer. Sometimes, we just don't care to move on and our potential becomes stagnated in a slew of despondency. It has happened to me. But, not for long.

If I blamed everything on my father, if I allowed myself to be kept down, I would never have gone anywhere. I would probably still be in Germany. I could easily have said: *he beat me, I can't do anything, I have no self-esteem and I can't make it.*

It is an easy thing to say that the answer to life's problems is to pull yourself up by your bootstraps. But as someone who actually has pulled herself up by her bootstraps, I believe I have the right to say it. Some people find that it is difficult to argue with the results of my mindset, even if it is easier said than done. I like to explain to people that, if one wants results, they ought to try not to make excuses.

I believe that, often, people make the mistake of reliving their past. It's not a healthy habit. The end result is that they eat themselves up inside. It may even begin to affect their health, both physically and emotionally. The next thing you know, you see them out on a street corner with no food and no home to go to. People need to look past what has already happened – it's in the past. I encourage them to use their energy instead, to make a better future for themselves.

For the sake of survival, never mind success, there is no replacement for a positive outlook and optimism for the future. Attitude makes all the difference; it is the difference between success and failure, the difference between poverty and wealth, the difference between a piece of coal and a diamond.

One needs to live life positively. Bad stuff happens. But we have to get over it. My advice to someone is always this: *don't use things as a crutch and don't hold grudges against people*; that won't get you anywhere. I believe that my childhood experience made me stronger. I wish it hadn't happened that way, but no one can change their past. I always knew I could do better, if only I chose to move forward, rather than dwelling on the past.

It would be inaccurate to say that I never received help from anyone, or to claim that nothing has ever gone my way. Yet, upon further reflection, there are a few able-bodied people in the world who cannot say the same. Instead of accepting their situation, they use it as an excuse and don't remember those who have helped them.

The fact is that it is easy for most of us to fold under far less pressure, to be crippled by our problems – headaches, which most likely the less-fortunate would be only too happy to suffer through. I have undergone tragedy, trials and tribulations, but I am still able to thank my lucky stars and to keep an optimism which came from my faith.

I was raised as a Catholic. These days, I don't go to church, but I still have faith. That's important. One must believe that everything happens for a reason and that you must simply keep going, no matter what. Always look forward. This is something that cannot be overstated. If I hadn't done that, I don't know what would have happened to me. The alternative might have been a street corner in a cardboard box, or reliance upon drugs or alcohol.

We must be grateful for what we have. We must make the most of it. I could be resentful of my childhood, but I truly do believe it made me stronger. I could be resentful of my ex-husband, but I am thankful for him instead. If it were not for him, I would not have come to America.

CHAPTER FOUR

NEVER GIVE UP

Despite a dismal early life, and an unhappy upbringing, I had a source of encouragement in my dear grandmother *Oma*.

"Don't worry about Renata, she will make it," I would overhear her say. She saw me cooking, cleaning, sewing, and helping around the house and she knew I had the right stuff. She always singled me out to my mother, praising me for all I did.

To an impressionable youngster, such praise went a long way in cementing a valuation of hard work and a high regard for self-sufficiency. Though my father would, at times, beat me, I always managed to maintain a sense of self-esteem through my grandmother's encouragement and strict work ethic.

If I couldn't do something, I wouldn't quit, I would learn how to do it. It became part of my personality to be a hard worker – always in possession of a can-do attitude. Just as my grandmother used to tell my mother, "With Renata's attitude, she will make it a long way in this life." She always made me feel so proud of myself.

Her encouragement followed through outside of the home also. I always made high marks in school, receiving grades of *Dobry* and *Bardzo Dobry*, or in English, *Good,* and *Very Good.*

[Insert Picture of Report Card]

Backed by my grandmother, I developed a strong sense of ambition at a young age. I had goals even before moving to Germany. I believed that my life as it was then couldn't be all there was and resolved not to live it out under the control of a drunken father. I told myself that I would be going places.

Today, I know that anyone can attain their goals, if they *never say never*. If one makes up their mind and works their heart out for it, they will succeed.

Notwithstanding his customarily unrestrained temperament, my father was, however, never in the regular habit of laying a violent hand on my mother. To my recollection there was only one exception, and that served as the straw that broke the camel's back.

I had already realized that it was not safe to live with my parents. I needed to leave, even though I was only seventeen. My father, despite everything, had never touched my mother. That day, when he did try to hurt her, I resolved not to live with it anymore. I resolved that I needed to get out of there, it was time to take care of myself. *You've got to move out*, I told myself.

By this time, as previously noted, I had a firmly-established sense of self-sufficiency and worth. That didn't mean it would be easy-going, however. I was a minor. Consequently, I was prohibited from legally renting an apartment and was generally hampered in most of the necessities for independence. Yet, moving out was hardly optional.

I did have a friend in a similar quandary though. He, too, was only seventeen and wanted to be out on his own. Together, we hatched a plan. Unless co-signed by parents or legal guardians, it was impossible to sign a lease to rent an apartment...unless, as the law stated, the renters were a married couple. This marriage, I admit, was only to be a marriage of convenience. But, at the time, it worked for both of us. Otherwise, neither of us had much interest in each other.

My new husband had, at the time, considered joining the military. The German Army provided stipends to subsidized housing for married enlistees. This gave two youngsters, who might otherwise have had no way to provide for themselves, double the impetus for marriage. It would be hard-going getting on our feet, but we were able to help each other as we went along.

I was not sure, at the time, where life would take me. For sure, I knew

I wanted to go places, and I knew that whatever awaited me, I could never get there without taking responsibility for myself.

This meant taking chances. Separating myself from an abusive household was the first step, and it was truly a step of faith. In some ways, true, it was an obvious choice to remove myself from such a negative situation. I knew what I was leaving behind, and the future looked bright in contrast.

However, taking a step into the adult world as little more than a child, I could not have known what awaited me. Upon reflection, fear of the unknown, anxiety, and apathy proved too much for my other siblings. They did not have the wherewithal to follow in my footsteps. Certainly, fear of the unknown might be natural, but allowing oneself to be overcome by that fear is not a positive attribute to me, and it is certainly not an attribute of mine.

CHAPTER FIVE

DRUG SMUGGLING

Back to the winter of 1982 in New York City, and my arrival at John F. Kennedy International Airport at seven months pregnant, it need hardly be said that I did not die in a fiery blaze. No bomb exploded. Although the passengers experienced an anxiety all too real, it would be discovered days later, that the bomb threat was nothing but a hoax. The perpetrator was none other than the affable, mild-mannered gentleman who sat beside me on the plane.

A bus came out to meet us imperiled voyagers, who were in haste to exit the threatened plane. With a sigh of relief, we made our way down the runway towards the terminal. The snow had let up for now, but I was hardly out of the woods yet. As I was about to learn, life as a seven-month pregnant drug-smuggler wasn't going to be so easy.

I was eager to make the final flight from New York to Boston. I was also eager to meet my husband's family. Above all, I was eager to bring this long and uncomfortable journey to an end. For this to happen, the first order of business was to be processed by immigration.

Entering the terminal, I was directed to the Immigration and Customs Center. Frank, because he was an American citizen, was cleared instantly. However, I was separated from him for the typical cross-examination needed to rubber-stamp a visa.

I was taken to a desk, where an expressionless, heavily built, and mustached middle-aged immigration officer sat. Although it was his duty to identify a persona non grata, and to prevent their entry to the United States without scanning the appropriate papers, he seemed altogether too sleepy to discover any irregularities in said paperwork. In a droning voice, he began a string of the typical questions, with a nonchalance that communicated to me a sense of sheer boredom and indifference, as if he couldn't care less what answers I might give.

"Why are you visiting America?" he asked.

"To be with my husband."

"Is your husband an American?" he asked in monotone.

"Yes."

"Why was your husband in Germany?"

"For business."

I wondered why I had to give answers to questions which I had already filled out in my visa application.

"Where in the United States will you be travelling?" asked the officer.

"To my husband's parent's house, I believe."

In my haste to leave Germany, I had not been bothered to worry about the details of where I was going. I knew that Frank had a handle on things, and I believed that would be enough for us.

"Where is that? Your husband's parent's house?" the officer qualified his previous question.

Now I was stumped. I knew that Boston was my next stop, but I did not know the town or street address of my final destination. There had been no reason to, until this time.

"I'm not sure."

I answered truthfully and, for the first time, the officer seemed to wake up. His eyes opened a little wider, showing a glint of suspicion, as if he had just caught on to something.

"Mrs. Keller," he said, "I am going to have to ask you to wait before we can clear you for entry into the United States. We just need to ask you a few more questions."

I was escorted around the corner to a small room that only held a few chairs, a table, and a telephone. There, I was left alone, and almost an hour went by before two new immigration officers entered, bearing a stack of papers and stern faces.

"You must understand that it seems very suspicious for someone to fly halfway across the world, and not know where they are going. It sets off some red flags that we will have to look into," said one of the officers.

"It makes us wonder what is really going on here," said the other. "Are you involved in any illegal activities – like drug smuggling for an example? We will find out everything. We have to be sure, before we can let you go."

I was horrified. *Of course I'm not a drug smuggler!* I thought to myself, *why would they ever think that?* At that point, I thought the best thing to do was to just keep quiet. The more I protested the more they would think I was guilty, I reasoned.

Yet, over the next couple of hours, the two officers cross interrogated me ad nauseam. They went over my application form with a fine-toothed comb. They asked me the same questions backwards and forwards. As the investigation dragged on, they even asked me trick questions to try and trip me up. It was a long, drawn-out and confusing experience for this tired mother-to-be.

"What is the address of your husband's family?" they asked repeatedly, as if I would/could somehow remember. Perhaps they thought I would make up an address, and they would catch me out. I don't know. I kept telling them, *I don't know! Get Frank in here. He can tell you.*

After a while, it became apparent that the immigration officers weren't fooling around; they really did believe that I was involved in some kind of drug-smuggling ring. Their rationale has mystified me to this day. Perhaps they had received information concerning a drug mule that fit my description. One can only guess.

After three hours of making no headway, one of the officers finally decided to call the number that I had listed as my contact information. It was Frank's mother's telephone number.

"We are going to call to see if your story checks out," one of the officers announced.

I reminded him, as I had done for hours, that they could verify everything by talking to Frank. Nevertheless, the officer proceeded to dial the number. The phone rang, and the officer began to speak.

"Hello," he said, "I am with the Immigration and Customs office at John F. Kennedy Airport. We have a person here who claims to be your daughter-in-law. We just wanted to call to make sure you are expecting her. We have some questions about her and wanna see that everything checks out. Could you help us make sure she's not involved in illicit drug smuggling into the United States? We believe that she may have drugs on her person. Could please tell me your street address, so we can confirm..."

He cut short, mid-sentence. Across the room, I could hear the buzzing dial tone. My mother-in-law had hung up on the officer. As might well be imagined, this made everything worse.

"She said she has never met you, and that she doesn't know you," the officer said in a foreboding tone.

Finally, I began to plead with my captors. I was beginning to feel trapped.

"Please bring Frank in here," I begged. "He can tell you everything. It is the house he grew up in, for goodness sakes. I am sure he can give you the street address."

With a reluctance that continued to confound me, they finally agreed.

All the while, Frank had been held outside the room, prevented from seeing me. He entered and began conversing with the authorities in English. Within a couple of minutes, he had told them our destination, address, and verified a few other facts. At long last, Immigrations and Customs allowed me entry to the United States. It was the end of hours of misery; the culmination of every traveler's nightmare.

Later, I would learn that my mother-in-law had misunderstood the situation, and decided not to help or support any 'drug users', whether they were her daughter-in-law or not. It was the beginning of an uneasy relationship.

These many years later, I remember my first troubling hours in the land that would become my new home. Sometimes, I think that if someone else were telling it, I would not believe my own life story. But it's the truth, I lived through it. I can see the irony of it all. Yet, more importantly, I can laugh about it now.

But the most amusing part for me, thinking about it all these years later, is that I never did find out what had motivated my neighbor in the plane to plan a bomb hoax! I had spent so much time with Immigration, I had missed my chance to question what had happened. To this day I have wondered about it. What could have possessed him? What a great story that would have made.

CHAPTER SIX

FRANK AND CARLO

By now, you will have realized that Frank is not my first husband. You will recall that I married for the sake of convenience before. That man was my own age. Dieter, a German youth intent on getting a jump on life through military service. How then did I find myself married to an American, and what circumstances had led me to flee to America? The answer to these questions began years before that frenzied flight to America.

Striking out in the world as a youngster, I found myself in search of a better life. My intuition told me that, rather than waiting for some unforeseeable turn of luck, I would be better served by building a career for myself and making my own fortune. A few short years went by before I found myself in the fevered corporate atmosphere of Frankfurt, working in the high-powered financial industry as a sales-woman. I found employment at a company that dealt in futures and commodities.

One day, I learned that there was to be a new sales manager, a hot-shot American broker and power-salesman named Frank Keller. Frank came with high commendations and soon proved himself a reliable go-getter at his new position. Frank lived big too. He drove a red sports car and projected a confidence, which soon attracted me to him.

It became apparent, before long, that Frank had his eye on me too; clearly impressed by my youth and vigor. It was recognized throughout the office that Frank was actively pursuing me, often taking lunch with me and going out of his way to impress. Increasingly, we spent time together, enjoying each other's company. After work, Frank would sometimes buy me a drink, and it was not long before I invited him home; a twenty-five minute commute to the outskirts of Frankfurt.

Frank met my husband Dieter, and initially did his best to maintain a cordial relationship with him, despite his less-than-secret wish to win me over. Frank offered to bring Dieter into the investment company, and soon we all worked together. All seemed to go along swimmingly. A conflict, however, was imminent; Frank knew that his relationship with me could go nowhere – so long as Dieter was in the picture.

Living as I did, so far from the office, I invited Frank to stay overnight at our apartment on the occasions that his visits lasted into the night. One such evening would serve as a turning point in my life. Thirty years later, Frank would recall, "It sounds like something out of a book or a movie, but it really happened."

Frank threatened Dieter with physical harm but did not touch him thank goodness. Amid the heated words Frank announced in earnest, "You don't deserve her unless you are willing to die for her."

"And," today Frank remembered, "I meant it."

That, as they say, was that. Dieter grabbed a few of his belongings and went on his way. Soon thereafter, the divorce followed.

Frank and I moved into an upscale hotel downtown and enjoyed the life that Frank's ample finances afforded. We attended parties and visited exclusive discos high atop skyscrapers. Frank received an offer to join a new company on the other side of Frankfurt, complete with a signing bonus, and made short work of leading sales at his new job. Conveniently, I obtained a job working in the same office.

Everything was on a roll and, in the magic of the moment, our relationship grew all the more serious. Before long, I was happy to learn I would soon be a mother. But it was a happiness which was not to last, for I experienced the terrible pain of miscarriage.

Frank tried to console me with a puppy; a delightful Cocker Spaniel that we named Carlo Von Sachsenhausen, as a joke. Carlo came complete with a full bag of tricks.

He could speak, shake hands, rollover and, one of his most clever tricks, he could destroy the white leather seats of Frank's factory-fresh, Mercedes SL 500 convertible. The stains never came out.

The three of us then moved into a new apartment and commenced spending money, as Frank would often say…"as if it were our hobby." We could spend two- three- four-thousand dollars on a weekend. Frank never worried about it. We often traveled on the weekends, touring much of Europe, including Spain, Switzerland and Greece. As we traveled abroad, Frank bought me expensive handbags, which Carlo obligingly tore to shreds. Everything seemed perfect. Frank and I lived in a daze, never thinking about tomorrow.

We were married on the second of April. Frank and I went to see a Justice of the Peace on the first of April (April fool's day). The Justice of the Peace said, 'There is no way that I will let anyone be married on April Fools. Come back tomorrow." So we did, and we were married April second.

Soon, I was pregnant again. For a short time, it seemed that everything was going to be just fine. My unfortunate upbringing and the hardships I had faced early in my adulthood seemed to fade into the past. The abuse of my father, the stark realities of moving out on my own as a minor, the confusion of a marriage of convenience-turned-inconvenient, all these things began to feel distant in contrast to what seemed a stable and brighter future. But all was about to come crashing down. Sometimes, what seems too good to be true, usually is.

CHAPTER SEVEN

THE ESCAPE

I want to affirm here that Frank is not a bad guy. He got involved with the wrong people and he was at the wrong place, at the wrong time. Unfortunately, he looked for shortcuts to succeed in business. Nevertheless, I am indebted to him. I would not be where I am today were it not for him. In many ways, I don't blame him. I am thankful for him.

The new life that Frank and I had carved out together in Frankfurt was about to explode in a big way. Frank worked as the third-in-command at his new job. The two co-owners ultimately called the shots, however. Frank was the next rung down on the corporate ladder. He worked as a broker and the head of the sales department. In practice, though not in authority, Frank nevertheless acted like a partner in the company.

I used to tell Frank that I did not trust his business partners. It always seemed to me that they were using him. Frank used to say, *you don't know business, you don't know what you are talking about,* and then he would ignore me. To me, the owners of the company he worked for seemed like two slippery characters; untrustworthy.

My intuition proved correct.

Later, Frank would admit that he always seemed to make it to a certain level in business and then he would hit an invisible brick wall. Once he had reached that level, it was as if all the decisions and the mistakes that were made by others was what brought everything crashing down. He always thought that there would be another tomorrow, that things could and would work themselves out – it was always *next week, next month, or next year.* He was so caught up in making money every day and making sure that the people who worked with him were making money that he didn't notice what was going on around him. He didn't notice how things were not lining up, as far as futures and regulations go in the commodities market. He didn't notice that he was being used unmercifully.

Yet, Frank would always claim, "Renata was never involved in any of this. She was never even asked to be involved. She was never a part of any bad business deals, she was never mixed up with it. But she stuck with me through all the bad times."

In 1980s Germany, there was a massive crackdown on futures brokers. The laws changed, and many large-scale investigations took place. Some companies were shut down or fined heavily. Even some of the companies I had been involved in were investigated. Fortunately, I was not a party to anything of that nature at the time.

I began noticing that Frank had become quite nervous. With good reason, I would later find out.

Frank eventually discovered that one of the co-owners of the company had the responsibility of placing option orders into the market. But one day, he found that several orders had not been placed. He was very upset when he found out and confronted the person in charge. At this time, due to the recent widespread investigations, the company then came under scrutiny. The co-owner tried to place the orders that had not been completed, but it was too late and that is where the problems began.

Frank received news from the other owner that an investigation was about to begin and that it was possible the office would be raided. Accordingly, Frank and the co-owners took steps to protect themselves.

They rented a small office across the street from the real office and moved all of their files and paperwork over there. The regular office only operated with minimal personnel, and no one answered the phones.

Meanwhile, I was not immune to the strain of the situation. Although I was not involved in any criminal activities, I was by no means merely just a bystander. I was pregnant and the future looked bleak. I began to worry that the father of my child would see jail time, and I began contemplating the devastating effect that might hold for the future of our family.

Frank grew increasingly more paranoid by the day, as might be easily imagined. His fears were not alleviated when the owners were tipped off that the company was about to be raided by the authorities.

Frank and his business partners rushed to the office; not to circumvent the law but to protect themselves. They assumed that business would be held-up for days, if not weeks, and proceeded to empty the safe and remove their personal property from the premises. From that time on, Frank felt as if he were on the run and perpetually staring over his shoulder, making steps to avoid any and all police contact.

Of course, I was never on the run from anything. Nothing could be brought against me legally. Nevertheless, I remained uncertain what the future would hold – a bad position for any woman to be in, let alone several months pregnant.

So many times I thought: *run away, leave it all behind*. I did not have to put myself through what was happening.

One afternoon, the police showed up at my mother's home. They asked her where we were living.

Now, I was beginning to feel the pressure as heavily as Frank. But I believed strongly that, come what may, I would do whatever it took to make sure that my child would have a father in the picture. Because of this, I was along for the ride, and this meant following Frank's lead – for now.

Fearing impending arrest at almost any moment and unable to cope with the anxiety, Frank took to drinking heavily. In his disheveled state of mind, he decided to take more extreme steps, walking everywhere rather than driving, in order that his red Mercedes would not be spotted by the police. Eventually, it became clear that staying in Frankfurt was not an option. Because I was in no danger, I was able to return home to pack our bags. As Frank, the getaway driver, parked far down the block, I walked home to retrieve some of our belongings. Together, Frank, Carlo the dog and I took up residency in a hotel in the town of Friedberg, northeast of Frankfurt.

In Friedberg, Frank's nerves recovered enough for him to realize that it was necessary to take legal steps to protect himself and, in effect, to protect me as well. He contacted a lawyer in Frankfurt and met with him several times over the next few days. After discussing the details of the situation, Frank's role, and the monies involved, the lawyer made the suggestion that the best way to take the pressure off Frank would be to meet with the prosecution team in order to make a statement.

Of course, as both of us realized, this would mean running a serious risk of arrest. Nevertheless, in order to relieve the tension it was the only viable option... or was it?

CHAPTER EIGHT

MAKING DEALS

Frank contacted the prosecutor's office and agreed to meet with him, under the condition that he would be free to leave after the meeting.

Frank would tell me later, "I went to the meeting, I was very nervous, I was worried that they might try to hold me after the meeting. I made a statement. I answered the questions he asked me. After I had signed the statement, he said it was okay for me to leave, but that I ought to keep myself available."

Frank had learned that both of his business partners had been on the lam as well. A few days after his meeting with the prosecutor, to his horror, Frank discovered that one of his partners had been arrested, was facing criminal charges, and would likely see jail.

At this time, we decided the best thing to do was to get out of the country as soon as possible. We met with Frank's lawyer, who was holding some money in escrow that Frank had given to him previously, and he agreed to give us back the money, minus his fee of course.

Then Frank began to work in earnest on how we could get out of Germany. He made lengthy and costly phone calls to his parents in Massachusetts, and began to prepare the paperwork necessary for me to go with him.

But now I faced a crisis: would I move to the United States with Frank, away from my family and everything that I knew? What was the necessity? Almost everything pointed against the idea. I was not in any trouble myself, so I felt there was no need to flee. I could, if I chose, stay in Germany and live my own life, separate from the *Sword of Damocles* which hung over my head so long as I continued to live with a wanted man.

Unfortunately, my family gave me no support. My sisters ridiculed me for even considering a move to America. My mother, now divorced from father, tried to persuade me that I did not need a man, especially one as troublesome as Frank.

"Stay here, in Germany," mother pleaded. "We can raise your child here, don't go to America."

But for me, the decision came down to one thing: Was it possible that I could allow my unborn child to be raised without a father in the picture? Despite everything, despite my own unhappy relationship with my father, despite the inconvenience of traveling and moving while seven months pregnant, and despite the vast sea of unknowns that awaited me in America, I chose to stay with Frank.

This decision was all the more remarkable, considering Frank's present state; he was a wreck. All the anxiety he had hoped to avoid by meeting with the prosecutor had returned full-swing. As he made phone calls, planned our traveling details and filed paperwork, he continued to drink heavily. All this notwithstanding, the necessary preparations were made and we prepared to make our escape.

With a warrant now out for Frank's arrest, flying from Germany was out of the question. The concentration of policemen and airport security made an arrest almost a certainty. Thus, we decided to make our way to Switzerland, where Frank could board a flight without scrutiny. Frank, the dog, and I were soon all aboard the night train to Zurich.

Nearing the Swiss-German border, tension mounted as the German conductors came through to check tickets. Frank feared his picture might have been posted by the police, putting him in danger of being discovered. But he also knew that the investigation of his company could not be escalated into an Interpol case in such a short time. Furthermore, Frank's lawyer had assured him that there was no danger of extradition once he returned to the United States. It was with much relief that we passed into Switzerland and free from danger.

Yet, I still maintained a feeling of apprehension. By traveling to America, Frank was, in a sense, going home. This was not at all the case for me, however. As the trip progressed, I began to wonder all the more what lay in store for me. After a brief stay in Zurich, we boarded a flight to New York City. I was lucky to be aboard at all, since I was seven-and-a-half months pregnant.

PART TWO

CHAPTER NINE

ALONG COMES JOHN

The winds of the Nor'easter roared on during that winter of 1982, as the plane lifted off from JFK. It was the final leg of the journey, which had begun in Frankfurt, Germany, and passed through Switzerland and New York City en route to Boston, Massachusetts. The flight was short and altogether unremarkable, which, as might be imagined, was a relief after the nightmarish ordeal in New York. As we landed, the snow began to fall all the more heavily with no sign of letting up. The pilot remarked that we had made it just in time; that flights were sure to be grounded for the next few hours.

We exited the plane and sought out our luggage, which also included a pet carrier for our little cocker spaniel, Carlo. By the time we had retrieved our belongings, it was already late in the evening. The interrogation had taken half the day and now it was almost ten o'clock in the evening. Something else was bothering me. I suddenly realized that something was missing. "Where is your family?" I asked Frank. "I thought the family would come to greet us." I began to have an inkling of what would soon become an uneasy relationship with my mother-in-law.

I was afraid, perhaps, my mother-in-law would bear me ill-will. Although, it seemed the authorities at JFK might have misled Frank's mother into thinking I was involved with drug trafficking, and her reaction over the phone seemed neither worried nor helpful. Most mothers-in-law, I believed, would instantly seek to help their daughters-in-law in a tight situation, even if there were some suspicion of illegal involvement. All the authorities wanted, after all, was to verify an address. I suddenly realized that I didn't even know this woman. I was certainly not starting off on the right foot. As Frank made some phone calls, I refused to let doubt set in, even after finding out regardless of the weather, that no-one in Frank's family had made plans to meet us. We were, for all intents and purposes, stranded. Then Frank got the idea of calling his uncle who lived in Seabrook, New Hampshire – a forty-five minute trip north of Boston.

Although Uncle Bob was a little grumpy because Frank had woken him up, he obligingly agreed to give us poor, weary travelers a place to stay. He was not able to pick us up, in light of the storm, however. Fortunately, we were able to find a taxi driver who was willing to take us, and we finally made our way north.

Uncle Bob was kind enough to allow us (including Carlo) to stay for the next couple of weeks. Uncle Bob was to play a pivotal role in my life and today, I remember him with much fondness.

At this time, I had no green card, and thus I was in danger of eventual deportation at the expiration of my original visa. In order to obtain a green card to become a legal, long-term resident, I would need to be sponsored by someone. Most times a new immigrant's sponsor would naturally be their spouse, if they were already an American citizen. But in this case, Frank was disqualified from sponsorship because the sponsor must be capable of providing for the immigrant. Frank did not have a job at the time, and thus could not prove that he was capable of providing for me.

Uncle Bob did not know me at all, beyond what Frank had told him about me, but he agreed to help with the green card. He didn't know if I was a lazy, no-good, conniving woman, but he generously agreed to help. For all he knew, he might have needed to support me.

From that time on, Uncle Bob and I were fast friends. Years later, when he died, I gave the Eulogy at his funeral and made sure to let everyone know that I was there – right at that moment – because of what this man had done for me.

Frank and I were, in a sense, stranded at Uncle Bob's. We had no car, no source of income, and no immediate outlets for work. Although always resourceful, I was limited in contributing to a better situation. I did not know English, I did not know American customs or business habits, and, on top of everything, I was going to give birth within the next couple of weeks.

Something had to be done. Uncle Bob was welcoming, but his small house was no place for a baby. With these many pressures ever on our mind, we decided to move closer to the rest of Frank's family. And so, with many thanks to Uncle Bob, we grabbed up our few belongings and the ever-loyal Carlo and relocated. We moved to western Massachusetts, to the town of Holyoke where Frank had grown up. In Holyoke, we rented a small apartment.

I believed that things were looking up. After our time on the run, Frank had calmed down significantly, and no longer suffered from the crippling panic attacks that had threatened to break up our relationship. I began to think that things would smooth themselves out soon, especially now that we were not alone in the world; we had Frank's mother and sisters to help get us settled in, and to make our new baby welcome in this new and hitherto unwelcoming land.

I already had quite a few reservations regarding my in-law's character. For one thing, there was the airport drug fiasco. Frank's mother, Martha, had shown a shocking lack of empathy in that crisis, and I wondered if she had only reacted poorly under strange and sudden circumstances, or if she was showing her true, somewhat selfish colors.

On top of the airport affair, I doubted my sisters-in-law as well. Why had none of them come to visit us? Why had they not made any steps to make their new sister – and for that matter, their own brother – welcome? I guessed that the news of Frank's unbecoming escape from Germany might have put them on edge against their brother, and by association, myself.

But now we were in Springfield, nearby Frank's family and a more familiar setting for the Keller family. I hoped my misgivings would be proven false. I always hoped to look on the bright side of any situation – but, by now, I knew how to plan for the worse. So many things in my life had gone from bad to worse, and now, even as I was about to experience the joy of welcoming my first child into the world, I found myself facing even harder times.

While Frank tried to get work and provide for our growing family, I stayed home in our apartment, incapacitated late in the third trimester of my pregnancy. I had nothing to do and no one to talk to. For one thing, I could not speak English, but on top of this, none of Frank's family ever came to visit. I found my mother-in-law to be a cold, uncaring individual, just as I had feared she might be. On the rare instances that I did encounter my in-laws, they showed a complete disinterest in me, and even a coldness towards Frank.

As already mentioned, we had almost no belongings, and few resources. We had no furnishings for our apartment. Now the problem was that I was about ready to burst, and we did not even have a bed to sleep on. I sat alone in the apartment, on a dilapidated reclining deck chair, with little else to do than stare at the walls. As I lay there, over time, the deck chair fell apart, and I had no relief. Only Carlo was around to keep me company.

In Germany, I did not have the ideal family, but it was still a family. At least I knew that I could rely on my mother and sisters, when bad came to worse. But with Frank's family, I had no such assurance. It seemed that Frank's family was at a completely different level of dysfunction.

The fact of the matter was that Martha Keller was affluent. She lived in a large house and their storage area was full of furniture, including beds and couches. What was more, she knew the state we were in but she showed no sympathy.

Martha was a self-centered woman. She had always lived in affluence and wished to be treated as a queen by her children. She played favorites, and enjoyed watching her children, particularly her daughters, attempt to curry favor with her. Frank was at the bottom of Martha's list of favored children, making me, by extension, even lower. There was only one way to stay in the good-graces of the old woman, and that was by buying her jewelry.

She cared for gold and diamonds more than anything or anyone. We had no money to buy her jewelry; we couldn't even afford to provide for ourselves.

Even when I tried to reach out to her, Martha showed no interest. She never worked to develop a relationship with me and, I found out later, it wasn't only because of the language barrier. Martha took a step further towards showing her animosity by making it known that she disliked Germans – plain and simple.

In the following weeks and months, I would witness my mother-in-law making gifts of furniture and other valuables to her favorite daughter. This only horrified me more. While the old woman knew of my plight and our uncomfortable situation, she chose to ignore me.

But my anger and frustration was short-lived. After all the turmoil, stress, and discomfort of the past months, I was overjoyed to welcome my first son, John, into the world.

CHAPTER TEN

HOME AGAIN

Some months had gone by, and I had only grown unhappier in America. I had a bouncing baby boy, true, but feelings of isolation had only grown stronger. Martha Keller remained cold towards me, as she would for the rest of her life. Frank tried to work as a used car salesman, and I had nothing to do but to stay home with John and Carlo, without any outlet for my energy and without any friends or family to speak with. Money was tight. Times were very different from the lavish living and familiar atmosphere of Frankfurt.

To me, the world seemed like a much less kinder place than it had been before. America held a lot in store for me but, for now, I had no way of knowing it. At this point in time, I was surrounded by a country of strangers. Soon, I began to feel terribly homesick. Unsure of what to do or how to cope, I determined I would return to Germany.

With so little expendable money, however, this was a challenge. For one-hundred and ninety-nine dollars, I booked a ticket from Iceland Air. Naturally, for that small sum, the flight was neither direct nor first-class. I would board a plane in Boston and fly to New York, where I would then board another plane to Iceland. Once in Iceland, I would make another long flight to Luxembourg. Landing in Luxembourg, I would then travel to Frankfurt by bus, which is an eight-hour trip. And, all this would be done with a baby still too small to walk.

I decided to take Carlo along for the ride too. I realized that Springfield was not the best place for a dog. None of the parks nearby allowed dogs. In my experience, dogs were allowed to go most places that people did in Germany. We had good friends, Peter, a lawyer, and his wife Mary, who had always admired Carlo and his many tricks, and so I decided that it was time Carlo moved to a better home. As it happened, the same couple had just bought a new Mercedes. They were overjoyed to hear the good news, but Peter remembered the infamous case of Frank's destroyed leather back seat, and opted to change out the seats from white to brown.

I was happy to return home to Frankfurt, but it was no pleasure cruise getting there. Getting from terminal to terminal was a chore, with a baby and little dog in tow. I was exhausted by the time I landed in New York. As the saying goes, *people are strange, when you're a stranger.* I was surrounded by strangers as I waited to board the flight to Iceland, and in my state of exhaustion, I began to worry. Sitting in a seat across from me at the terminal was a tall man, who kept stealing glances at baby John. I began to feel uncomfortable, and this feeling was compounded by the fact that the man was a middle-easterner, complete with the attire of his culture. Earlier that year, there had been several hijackings, and I could not help but feel suspicious. It seemed to me that this middle-easterner was a little too interested in my baby.

Although I felt a little uneasy at first, I chose to ignore my gut-feeling for the time being. But my apprehension returned when I boarded the plane and found that I was seated immediately next to this foreign, seemingly-ominous man. The plane took off, as did my anxiety.

The flight continued as expected. Then, to my dread, only ten minutes into the flight, I realized that I needed to use the bathroom. I could not take my baby with me to the small bathroom onboard the plane. John sat there in his baby carrier beside me as good as you please. I was nervous, but I didn't want to make a scene, and so I decided to leave him for a moment and rush off to the lavatory in the rear of the plane. When I reached the lavatory, I realized that there was a short line so there was nothing to do but wait.

A few short minutes later, I returned to my seat where a shock awaited me. I found the strange man was holding my baby. Despite trying to hold in my fear, my maternal instincts took hold and I could not help but take the offensive.

"Why are you holding my baby?" I asked angrily.

"Oh," the man replied in German, "He was crying, so I picked him up and tried to feed him his bottle."

He turned out to be the nicest guy. He offered to hold the baby while I took a nap, and even asked if I would prefer the window seat. I felt terrible for having been afraid and even more so for having judged him. We had friendly conversation for the rest of the journey. That's when I learned that you can't judge a book by its cover. I made a mistake thinking that way. I have learned from that experience. You can never tell. It's best to treat everyone with respect, and not judge people you don't know.

With this false alarm over, I continued the rest of my tiresome journey without event. Back home in Frankfurt, I was refreshed to see my family, who were also very happy to see our baby boy. It was nice to see familiar faces, and to understand and converse with the people around me. Mother began to encourage me to stay in Germany. My sisters told me that I would not make it in America, and that I might as well stay in Frankfurt. I was faced with a hard question: should I return to Frank and America?

Just as had been the case before, I believed that a child ought to be near its father, if at all possible. I knew that America held many opportunities that John might one day be able to take advantage of. It might not be comfortable living in America just yet, but it seemed like the right decision to make. I was never one to take the easy path. And so, paying no attention to my sisters' negativity, I enjoyed the rest of my vacation and returned to the United States.

CHAPTER ELEVEN

SESAME STREET

On top of the newfound difficulties of relocating to America was an overshadowing problem, which seemed to compound every other problem: I could not speak English.

When I was in high school, living in Germany, there were English classes, but I never paid attention. I never thought I would need English.

Certainly, it was not in my plans to ever move to America. For one thing, there was a general public view in Western Germany that although America was our ally in the Cold War, Americans were, nevertheless, outsiders who did not really belong in Germany. There was also a view that Americans were troublemakers and had something of an arrogant attitude. It wouldn't be too strong to say that many Germans viewed Americans as being, perhaps, a little obnoxious. Because of this, when I was younger, I never felt that I wanted anything to do with Americans, and I never took the trouble to learn English.

Evidently, there were plenty of young German women at the time, who felt differently. It was a common thing to hear about girls who would marry American men on-the-quick, or as a sort of mail-order bride, to get American citizenship. But I never thought very highly of that, and never considered it as an option for myself.

Yet there I was, not only married to an American, but living in America, with a son who was an American citizen as well.

It was now a little over a year after I had arrived in America. We lived in Westfield by this time, nearby Frank's immediate family. John was getting older, crawling and learning to walk. On warm spring days, I would walk him to a nearby playground. Many other mothers did the same, and they chatted pleasantly with each other as our children played together. They didn't seem to have a care in the world. However, I could only stand there and smile, surrounded by people who might be my friends, were it not for the language barrier.

After a few days of this, I began to feel humiliated for not fitting in; isolated with no one to talk to. Frank's mother and sisters seldom visited, despite my encouragement. It was not long before I began to entertain the idea of moving back to Germany. After all, things had not panned out ideally thus far in America. I remembered a conversation I had held with my mother, before I left Germany.

"Don't go to America," my mother had said. "We can raise your son here."

But I also remembered an unkind declaration my elder sister had made.

"We will see you again soon, I bet you anything," she had said, "you won't make it in America. I'll give you a couple of months, at best, before you are back here again."

But I was not the quitting type. I believed strongly, just as I had before leaving Germany, that it was important for a child to be with both parents. I also liked America, for the most part. The people were generally friendly and it seemed like a land of opportunity – if only I could learn English. Since Frank was gone most of the day, I was left to my own devices.

One bright and sunny day, I felt too despondent to take John to the playground. Instead, I sat him in front of the television to watch *Sesame Street*. It was a typical show, "brought to you by the letter 'A,'" and so on. Together, John and I sat there, watching intently, when suddenly, it hit me like a bolt from the blue. Although I had played the show several times before for John, I had never given it much thought. But now, I realized that the show was about the basics of the English language.

If kids could learn it, I can learn it, I told myself. For the next few weeks, I was sure to watch *Sesame Street* whenever it was broadcasted, usually three-times-a-day. It was all that I had at my disposal, so I made the most of it. *Sesame Street* might not have been an exhaustive course, but it gave me the basics, which was still miles ahead in practicality, and more than enough to boost my confidence. Today, I laugh about the true story of how Elmo helped me to learn English. So much has changed since then, but learning English was my first step towards becoming the self-made business woman that I am today.

Along with me, the world has changed so much. Some say the world is getting smaller every day. The Internet has given the 21st Century American a chance to learn about any subject, in any language they choose. I did not have the Internet, but I did have a can-do attitude, and with a can-do attitude even something as commonplace as a children's television show can become an opportunity. Although circumstances seemed harsh, although I felt isolated and friendless in an unfamiliar country, I never succumbed. I never stopped believing that I could find a way to make it through the hard times.

Empowered by my new know-how, I found the confidence to seek out a job.

I see the owner of a certain donut shop every now and then, bringing to mind my first job in America. The last time I saw him he told me, "When you first started working, you couldn't even string a sentence together."

I might have struggled at the beginning, but I was honest and hardworking, and there was never a penny missing at check-out time.

With increased exposure to new workplaces, my grasp of the English language grew, and further opportunities became available. When we relocated to the opposite side of the state of Massachusetts to the town of Reading, I took on new jobs in manufacturing and worked in coffee and donut shops, while Frank worked as a part-time car salesman. The future looked promising for me. Frank had a new plan, and it seemed that soon money would be pouring in, as it had before.

CHAPTER TWELVE

UNDESIRABLE ASSOCIATE

After a while, Frank and I decided to take our hard-learned skills in investment and sales and reapply them in a new venture. Frank was wary of re-entering the futures market because of our experience in Germany. But his work in commodities led him to believe that gold could be an excellent outlet for investors. Together, we started our own business buying and selling rare and valuable coins and gold pieces. I managed the office while Frank worked his magic on the phones. Before long, we had opened an office in Hampton, New Hampshire and had six new salesmen under our employ.

"Without patting myself on the back too much," Frank related, "I believe it is safe to say that I was one of the best phone salesman in the United States at the time. I once held a record for the highest single-call sale. One call, one close, the money was wired the next day, one-hundred-and-fifty-six thousand dollars."

The success we experienced in the rare coin industry was centered on Frank's sales approach.

"My philosophy is this: it's all about telling a story. If one is selling high-ticket investments, you need to have the real inside scoop. Every rare coin has its narrative –its history, its grade, how many were minted, its range of values, and so on. If I had a fascinating story, I would use it as my approach in selling. I would tell people where they could find the information on each particular sale, I would tell them to do their research, and they would buy. Before long, I found that there was little need for the buyers to actually see what they were buying in person."

As an example, Frank's best sell ever was a Double Pan Pacific pure-gold set, signed by President Theodore Roosevelt. There were only ten sets ever minted, and they were dispersed throughout the world.

If given the opportunity, Frank could take a line like that straight to the bank. With his approach, the company took off. Money flowed in, and Frank indulged me with a gold watch and other jewelry. Soon we began selling inventory as fast as we could lay our hands on it. Things were looking up all the time, but for these opportunities to continue, the company required a better inventory.

Frank was a good salesman, but he always wanted to get rich fast. It had to be today, not tomorrow. He might still be in business today if he'd remembered that a successful business takes time to build up, but he always wanted more…

Years later, my business success is based on the principles of hard work and frugality. I don't need to make millions of dollars instantly. I believe in investing in the right places and working hard.

Soon our company partnered with a long-established rare coin company in Saugus, Massachusetts, which boasted a stellar business reputation, and had one of the finest inventories in the United States. Frank hit it off well with the owners of the company, brothers Fred and Mark.

But now we recognized a logistical problem. They were selling at a different location than where the merchandise was held. This became a problem for delivery, and on the occasion that a customer demanded to see a piece before buying. Consequently, we decided to move the business operation from Hampton, New Hampshire to Saugus, Massachusetts, taking our salesmen with us. As it happened, we moved in with the company in which we had partnered, renting a second-story space in the same building.

Later, we also moved into a larger house, in nearby Reading, Massachusetts. This was partly due to the fact that I was pregnant again with our second son. Everything seemed to be improving for the better.

Then a problem arose: cash flow slowed to a trickle.

The best salesman (after Frank) had a cocaine habit that often interfered with his work. Although he was able to bring in the sales, he was an inconsistent worker, often disappearing for days at a time. Additionally, the other salesmen hit a slump, underperformed and did not bring in the deals. With the weight of the company resting primarily on Frank, cash-flow problems soon seemed an almost insurmountable obstacle.

We provided salaries for six salesmen, as well as holding a large overhead. Because of the nature of the company, the phone bills would often run as high as a thousand dollars a month. In addition, there was rent, other costs, and dues owed to our partners.

The same problem which Frank had experienced in Germany cropped up again. All the salespeople used him. As I sat in the office, I saw how people took advantage of him. Frank always wanted to make a big show and he trusted everyone. But he was the boss, he should have used more caution.

"I need you to forward me my next paycheck, I need the money." "I have a big deal in the works, it will come through, but I need the money to live on."

Yeah, right. They never closed the deals, and then Frank would get stuck. He was the boss, he should not have let them work him over like that.

Undeterred by underperforming employees, Frank stayed on the ball in sales. He often depended on what is known in the sales business as *loading*. He would rely on repeated customers with which he had a proven relationship, in order to move inventory and free up cash flow. But as the main breadwinner, pressures mounted and the bills stacked up. Business was in the red, and we began to owe money right and left. We were fighting a losing battle, but it seemed that Frank might have had a stroke of luck.

Frank had a client, Pedro, with whom he had built a friendly relationship over the past couple of years.

When I first met Pedro, I figured out right away that he was a shady character. But Frank didn't want to hear it. I told Frank that he was making a big mistake, that Pedro was nothing but trouble. Frank went right ahead and did business with him regardless.

From time to time, they would go out to lunch, usually discussing a business deal or two. One particular afternoon, Pedro asked Frank a commonplace question – one that is usually answered truthfully, or not, as "fine."

"How is business?" Pedro asked.

But Frank did not answer with *fine*.

"I've got some large deals on the horizon," Frank admitted, "But, I haven't been able to put them together, and I need them to happen right now."

Because Pedro was on such friendly terms, and he had found Frank to be a reliable businessman, he inquired if Frank could use any financial help.

"How much would you need, right now, to make it until you can pull these big deals through?"

"Between ten and twelve thousand dollars," Frank answered candidly.

"That's not a problem, I can get that for you," Pedro answered, as if it were nothing.

Meanwhile, I remained unaware of these goings on until after the fact. Yet, just as before, when we lived in Germany, I was not immune to the pressures of Frank's business decisions. Uncertainty was creeping up on us again, but this time much more was at stake. Now we had two young boys. Our second son James had been born a few months before, and this only served to amplify the financial pressures which we now faced.

A couple of days later, Frank and Pedro met once again, and Pedro handed Frank a thick roll of dollar bills wrapped in a rubber band.

"An alarm should have gone off, when I saw that big roll of cash," Frank recalls. "I should have known that exchanging money in that style did not bode well for the money's origin."

Nevertheless, Frank took the money and reinvested it in the company, covering the outstanding bills and allowing business to continue.

Frank knew that such a sizeable loan could easily be repaid when the deals went through.

My intuition, as it often did, told me that there was something not quite right with Pedro. I had voiced this opinion to Frank before, with no resulting answers. The next thing I knew, my family was receiving death threats.

CHAPTER THIRTEEN

THE MOB

The year is now 2012, and it was probably one of the most trying times of Frank's life. It was a period of hardship that eventually ended in our divorce.

As Frank said, "I went through hardships – unthinkable hardships – and I wasn't there. Not for my children. But I simply moved forward and somehow, I had the business smarts to manage money and all the other things that go into starting a company. This year marks a quarter of a century in business. I could never have predicted it. Not the Renata Plitzko I knew – or thought I knew. As they say: *When your back is up against the wall, you learn what metal a person is made of.* And she showed me that she was made of steel.

I would never have guessed that the Renata I knew in Frankfurt, Germany could have made it this far. True, she had a tough upbringing, but the real success story started when Renata was caught with no help, no support, and no family. She was left stranded, with two small children."

The trouble all stemmed from the loan that Frank, in a panicked state, had received with no questions asked from his friend Pedro.

Time went by, and the big deals which Frank had expected were not coming through. The twelve thousand dollar loan was long gone, and our company seemed as much a loss as it had been before. Nevertheless, Frank held out that things might still swing our way. But with the other salesmen continuing to underperform, there was nothing to be done but for the losses to be cut and employees to be let go.

After a couple of weeks of hard luck, Pedro called.

"Frank, what's the story?" he asked.

"The deals still haven't come through yet," Frank stated plainly.

"Okay," Pedro replied, "you told me they would have gone through by now, but I will wait a little longer."

Frank reflected that, "In business, it often happens that things don't quite pan out the way you had planned."

Some while later, Pedro called again and confronted Frank. He stated that he could wait no longer, he needed the money back and that was all there was to it. He gave Frank two more days, but circumstances did not change in that short time.

Three days later, I returned home to find Frank in a state of shock. Frank had been home with the two children when he heard a knock at the front door. Two men, neither of whom Frank recognized, had come to the door. They asked to come in, and it soon became quite apparent that they were not selling Bibles. They said that all they wanted to do was talk. Frank suspected that he knew what the topic of conversation would be but, once in doors, as the idiom goes, they got up in Frank's face.

One of them pushed Frank against the wall, while the other pulled out a gun and proceeded to put the barrel up against Frank's face. Around the corner, John and James played, unaware of the trauma their father was experiencing.

"We are going to give you forty-eight hours to get the money," the man with the gun said, giving Frank a look full of terrible meaning. "Remember, forty-eight hours, or we're coming back."

Frank was aware that the intruders knew that he had two small children in the next room, and this fact horrified him. He knew that he had to do something, not only to protect himself, but also to protect me and the two boys. For, as he knew by this point, the money in question was not Pedro's money. It was on loan from the mob, and that was nothing to fool around with.

The next day, we returned home to find a fire engine in our driveway and firemen crowding the front lawn. There was no fire, nor any other emergency; someone had called in a false alarm. But we both knew better than that: it was a threat.

Without telling me, Frank devised a plan. Time was running short. Desperate times call for desperate measures, and Frank thought he might have just the plan. Little did he know that it would land him in prison.

CHAPTER FOURTEEN

MISSING COINS

Frank called Pedro and presented him with his plan.

"Pedro," Frank said, "What if I were to give you a set of platinum coins, valued at almost twenty-five thousand dollars?"

Pedro was interested in the proposition and Frank told him more. "I can give you these coins to hold as collateral, until I am finally able to bring through the kind of deals I have been working on. Then I can pay you back."

It will be recalled that our company sold inventory for the company in Springfield with whom we had partnered. The second day after the home invasion, Frank made a sale and, consequently, accessed the safe where much of the inventory was held.

In some cases, the safe held gold and coins which had already been sold. Sometimes, customers opted to keep their purchases in the company vault – especially in a case where they were afraid to keep them at home. Frank decided to borrow from a stash of already-sold pieces, creating a situation where this supposed piece would be sold again. Using an already sold gold piece, it was less likely to be discovered in the short period of time before Frank could retrieve the piece back from Pedro, unless the owner discovered it missing in the meantime.

Frank picked out a set of particularly rare platinum coins, complete with a certificate which proved their value of approximately twenty-five thousand dollars, and made the hand-off to Pedro. In return, Pedro gave his word that he would hold the set, without selling it, until Frank could repay the loan.

The danger that the family faced would soon be a thing of the past, Frank surmised. The only thing to do now would be to make some big sales happen. But as I was about to learn, our luck had only turned for the worse. A disaster struck once again.

Frank's appendix ruptured, forcing him to drop everything. As days went by, the risk of the missing gold being discovered increased exponentially. Then one day, the worst thing that could have foreseeably happened, did. As Frank lay in his hospital bed slowly recovering Mark, the co-owner of the partnering gold company, came to visit.

Mark revealed that he'd discovered coins missing. The owner had inquired about them and they could not be found in the vault. Mark's company had never experienced anything so disastrous before. In fact, they had prided themselves on their clean business record. In the rare coin industry trust is crucial, needless-to-say. Twenty-five thousand dollars in missing merchandise was no laughing matter, and that is why he had come to see Frank.

In his panic, Frank fed him a line that the coins were not in the safe. This seemed good enough for the time being, and Frank realized that, regardless of his condition, he needed to get out of the hospital. The following morning, he signed himself out and got Pedro on the phone. The simple solution, Frank realized, would be to deliver the coins to the customer, safe and sound.

But to his dread and dismay, Frank learned that Pedro was no longer in possession of the set of coins. He had taken them and promptly sold them well below their market value, in order to quickly regain the cash which he had initially lost. Pedro had borrowed the money from a certain notorious Boston area mobster, and thus there was no way of ever retrieving the coins. Furthermore, Pedro added that if Frank ever revealed with whom he had done business, the whole family would pay for it.

CHAPTER FIFTEEN

PORTSMOUTH, NH

Frank was in big trouble now, and my children and I would pay the price.

What am I doing here, in America, with this man? I would often ask myself. *I could be in Germany. I would rather be in Germany.*

All the while, also thinking, *who would remain married to this man, after all the things that have happened. No-one, that's who! Or at least almost no one.* But things were more complicated now. I had two children to consider, and I could not just pick up and leave.

After arraignment, because of his hitherto clear record, Frank was released on a personal recognizance bond. A court date was set, but things did not look good for him. There was no future in Springfield or Reading. I had already began to take charge of the situation months before when the gold business had slowed to a halt.

I single-handedly moved our belongings when we were forced to downsize to an apartment in the town of Amesbury. I had picked up jobs in order to keep the family financially afloat. Fearing what future the impending legal proceedings held, Frank lived in a daze over the next couple of months. Despite the fact that he was not in the best physical or mental health, he attempted to provide for his family by working as a used car salesman. As it had before in Germany, his anxiety returned to its apex, leaving me as the glue to hold our lives together.

Although I took responsibility and did my best to maintain a positive attitude, times were tight in Amesbury. I worked on the third shift at a fuse manufacturing plant, but money was not the only problem. Long months of struggle had already taken its toll, and to top it all off, the impending doom of Frank facing jail time and me facing single-motherhood hung over our heads, like a poorly balance boulder that might come crashing down at any time.

Many times, I had encouraged Frank to keep business steady. It seemed to me that gradual improvement was the key to a steady business, not scheming for get-rich-quick deals. To this day I believe that, generally speaking, there are no shortcuts to success. Keeping one's nose to the grindstone will always trump trying to find shortcuts, in my estimation.

I had been put through the works with Frank. This is not to say that Frank had planned it that way, but it amounted to the same thing. As a result, our relationship struggled. The months before Frank's court date were full of a tension, which would end in the dissolution of our marriage.

In the meantime, Frank had taken up work once again as a used car salesman, and I had a car. One day, on my way to work, I noticed a billboard which advertised a new and affordable apartment complex in Portsmouth, New Hampshire. This discovery came in the nick of time. When I returned home, I learned that we had been served with an eviction notice and would be forced to leave.

The next day, as I passed the billboard once again, I took down the contact number and called the realtor in charge of the properties. In Frank's present state, it was up to me to take charge or my family might end up homeless.

The realtor took me to see the new apartments.

They were affordable and met our needs, so I signed the lease then and there. I went back to Amesbury and I told Frank that we were moving. Just like that. We were about to be out on the street and we needed to move out, and fast.

Unfortunately, in order to make the security deposit, it meant that I would have to part with every last bit of jewelry I owned.

When we worked in the rare coin business, Frank bought me a beautiful gold watch. I had to sell it far below its true value. I simply had to make it happen. You have to do what you have to do.

All told, I had just enough to make the security and one month's rent for the lease. We threw everything we owned in a U-Haul, and away we went to live in Portsmouth.

It seemed that I was building momentum. Where obstacles had presented themselves, I had transcended them. Over the past couple of years, I had overcome a language barrier, given birth to two children, leased an apartment, taken on jobs, and helped to provide for my family.

But now it seemed that all my momentum was about to come to an abrupt halt. Over the next few months, disaster would strike – yet again. Frank would be jailed, I would face racism and discrimination in the workplace, and I would go broke again faced with another eviction. But this time, as a single mother of two young boys.

CHAPTER SIXTEEN

GOODBYE FRANK

One day, we were home at the apartment at *The Pines* when two men appeared at the front door. They were investigators with the City of Portsmouth and they had arrived to escort Frank to court.

At court, Frank's lawyer arranged a plea-deal. He could go free if he would testify against Pedro and help to indict the other guilty parties. But in light of the mob's role, Frank realized that the two boys and I would likely be endangered if he chose this route.

Now I was alone. I had lived through good times and bad. I had suffered through crisis after crisis, and managed to come out unscathed. I had defied my family's expectations, but they had seen nothing of what was to come. After the Mercedes, the fur coats, the lavish living in upscale hotels and vacations abroad, after the gold watches and new life in what some would call the *land of opportunity*, I was left totally alone. I was responsible for two small children, both in diapers, and now it was I who must single-handedly bear on my shoulders the weight of the world.

"Wrap it up and come to Germany," my family said.

The more people who fed me that line, the more it served to harden my resolve. I would make it somehow. I just didn't know how at the time.

I could have hooked up with a rich, old man. I would later have plenty of opportunities for that.

But, what set me apart at this time was the way I handled and was able to overcome conflict.

I could be resentful of my Frank, but I am also thankful; if it were not for him, I would not have come to America.

I did not wallow in self-pity, nor did I want to blame Frank for everything. Instead, I chose to continue believing that everything happens for a reason, and that circumstances would work out so long as I kept my eyes on the future. Now, after twenty-five years alone in business, my resilience has paid off. My company is top-rated by the Better Business Bureau. If you happened to turn the radio on locally in the New Hampshire seacoast area, you might hear one of my advertisements.

"I am Renata Plitzko, and I approve this message."

Some might say that I have managed to steamroll every obstacle that has stood in my path merely by chance, or by some luck. Some would say that attitude has nothing to do with success; that achievements are all a result of the universe dealing one a better hand than their neighbor. It is a fatalism which people often buy into, perhaps in order to bolster their sense of self-worth despite their failures.

I know better. Anyone can change their stars. In a sense, I am a self-fulfilling prophetess. My achievements have occurred thanks only to my attitude. Consider for example: was I really born in the *right* country, into the *right* family? Did I really go to the *right* schools? Did I really marry the *right* guy, and settle down to the *right* job? No! None of those things.

When one realizes that they have the power to change the course of their life, it is at that precise time when they may truly capitalize on really good fortune when it comes around. After Frank was sent to prison, I would see crises once again. But this time, opportunities would present themselves and I would always seize the moment.

CHAPTER SEVENTEEN

SINGLE MOTHERHOOD

Before Frank was sent to jail, he took responsibility for paying the bills. When the rent bills came in the mail, Frank would tell me that he was taking care of them.

"The rent is taken care of, don't worry," he would say. But only after he was arrested, did I find out that we were three months behind in our rent.

Making matters worse, my car had broken down. I did not have enough money to fix it and I was in danger of losing my job. On top of this, I had no money to pay for a babysitter. In the past, Frank watched the children while I worked, but now this problem had presented itself adding to the stack of other outstanding bills.

With the rent three months behind, I faced eviction once again. In desperation, I contacted the landlord with whom I had never had much of a relationship before because he had always dealt with Frank – he was the man of the family.

I told him the whole situation. I told him how my husband had told me that he was paying the rent. I asked him to please give me a break and not to evict me. I told him that I have two small children; that I would work to get him the money and that I would make it happen. I would do whatever it took.

What happened next was truly remarkable, and continues to convince me that everything happens for a reason.

"I'll tell you a story," the landlord said. "When I was younger, I was in the Army. I was stationed in Germany for a couple of years. While I was there, I met the love of my life. I don't even know where she is today. I wish I did. I loved this woman so much, even all these years later, I still get sick over it. I miss her so terribly. I wanted to find her so I could marry her, but I never could. I would do anything to see her again. Absolutely anything..."

All this while, I wondered what the story had to do with me.

"Do you know what her name was?" the landlord asked. "It was... will believe in you. Because your name is Renata...for the sake of the other Renata I knew, I will give you a chance. You are lucky. Normally, I would not allow someone to stay after they are three months late."

I made good on my promise, and dutifully struggled to pay the back rent. Every extra five dollars I had, I would send the landlord's way.

I did not want to disappoint him for the opportunity he had given me. Within a couple of months, I made up all the back rent – everything – and was current on the rent. After a while, he knew that I would make good. He noticed I was so responsible with money, he eventually asked me if I wanted to buy the condo I was renting.

From that time on, I have made it my practice in life to dispatch bills immediately. I don't want to owe anybody anything. I hate owing people. I don't even have credit cards.

Frugality has come to be one of my hallmarks. Living within your means is important. We are living in an economic recession. Many people bought houses when they couldn't afford the mortgage payments. Now they are under foreclosure.

You see Americans driving around in these expensive BMWs and Mercedes. Sometimes people ask me, *Renata, you are German, why don't you drive a Mercedes?* I could afford a new BMW if I chose to buy one, but it is so unnecessary. Vanity, it would seem, is not a necessary ingredient for getting ahead. I drive a Scion, which is an inexpensive subsidiary of Toyota.

But responsibility with money was by no means the only issue that I would face. Although I had been lucky with my landlord, things were about to take a turn for the worse. Over the following months and years, I would experience the trials of single-motherhood and would suffer from malicious xenophobia and discrimination in the workplace. I would risk poverty, and my two sons would be endangered by a pedophile. How did I make it in America after all?

PART THREE

CHAPTER EIGHTEEN

A HOME AT LAST

Today, I live in the city of Portsmouth located on the seacoast of New Hampshire. A historic New England city, Portsmouth's founding dates back to 1653. Now, Portsmouth is a bustling center of culture and business, leaving me not without competition in my line of work.

Pulling up the driveway, my house reminds me of coffee and cream with its light-brown body and white trim. To a newcomer taking in the property, a few things immediately stand out. First, the symbols of my two-fold identity: two flags – the red, white and blue of America and the black, red and gold of Germany. The flags fly prominently and unapologetically. One could not drive by without sensing the presence of something of a dual-patriotism, or at least a dual-enthusiasm. I am both American and German. Although I am a naturalized American citizen, I cannot disown my German origin or ethnicity, nor would I wish to. I am a German-American and proud of it.

The house itself is in excellent repair, the paint job is recent, the windows are clean and, as a whole, I think the place looks neat and tidy. The second-story is a new addition. I've been told that one would never guess it was not original. Everything is as it should be, calling to mind the German orderliness of lore. I am proud to say that it is at once evident I take great pride in my property.

Then there is the landscaping. I keep the lawn immaculate and emerald-green, despite the fact that it is now September as I write this. Surrounding the house is a garden, complete with a goldfish pond, where frogs may be heard croaking contentedly. Almost in defiance of eminent autumn frosts, all manner of flowers bloom brightly; chrysanthemums, foxgloves, hydrangeas, and cosmos, to name a few.

I always wanted it to look like Prescott Park, the idyllic riverside gardens and the pride of Portsmouth.

Living in Poland as a girl, I worked in the pasturelands of Oberschlesien. Over the past few years, I have rediscovered my green thumb. Practically speaking, it is safe to say that my *green thumb* is less of the intangibility generally connoted by that term, and more of an investment of patience and a commitment of time. I think my labor of love is an improvement to the whole community. One cannot but surmise that my home is a realtor's dream, the kind of property that raises the entire neighborhood's appeal, I'm proud to say.

I love my house, but if somehow everything I own was taken away, I think I could still make it. I would grow my own food. I still have the survivor's mentality, something sometimes lost in the American quest for comfort, I believe.

I cleaned a lot of toilets for this. Nobody gave me this house. I am pleased and happy to say this.

After all I have been through, I would not wish to be handed anything. That is not the kind of person I am. I believe that my house is a pristine symbol of my work ethic, not merely a comfortable place to live. Yet, without the house I would still have 'the right stuff'. I know I would.

I am not a materialist. Take it all away, and I will be the same person. I am convinced of it.

To a certain degree, some of life is luck. But if one isn't willing to change to one's circumstances and step up when the need arises, they will never succeed.

Most would agree that my statement rings true in a general kind of way. But far from being a simple truth, this is central to the story of my life thus far. It was luck that brought me to the United States. I came to America at the spur of the moment, but since that time, it has been a long and difficult road. It is a road with a destination that some might call the *American Dream*; a beautiful home, a successful business that brought financial security. But progression was an uphill struggle; a road where I could have easily dropped to the ground and quit at any time. It is a road full of the epitaphs of quitters, but it is also a struggle that anyone can survive – with the right attitude.

The cynical among us, of course, might be tempted to discount my outlook on life. Voltaire's cynical masterpiece, *Candide*, famously mocks the kind of optimism that teaches *everything is for the best*. My answer is more sophisticated than what I feel is the naive view that everything negative will somehow turn positive.

Life is what you make of it. Don't waste your life with negativity.

In the Declaration of Independence of 1776, Thomas Jefferson famously penned the phrase, "Life, liberty, and the pursuit of happiness." It should be distinguished that Jefferson claimed the right *of* happiness, not a right *to* happiness.

If I have found the key to the *American Dream*, it was not through an instant rags-to-riches story, it is not because anything was given to me. It was through hard work and the *pursuit of,* in the proper meaning of the term. I believe that I deserve the gains from what I have worked for, and nothing more. There were no guarantees for the pregnant young German woman who left for America with nothing. There were no guarantees. But, where there's a will, there's a way. Where there was a positive outlook, there was opportunity.

Walking into my home, one will notice the interior of the house is as well-kept as the outdoors, with freshly painted walls and immaculate hardwood floors. I am humbled to say that many have admired my house. Only ten years after buying it, I can boast that my home is valued far above its modest previous price. I believe this is a noteworthy accomplishment, in light of the recent nationwide housing bubble and the consequent plummeting real estate value.

There is a recession, economically. But it is also a depression in the minds of people. That is why I want to tell my story, so people can hear that they can actually be successful if they live within their means, work hard, and just keep looking forward.

My message is one of hope and perseverance, of struggle and disappointment, and of a contagious, self-sustaining optimism.

I believe that everything really does happen for a reason. I fully believe it.

But how did I manage to make it through all my hardships to finally end up owning this beautiful house?

CHAPTER NINETEEN

JARED

By now, I had realized that there was no way that Frank and I could recover our relationship. It was obvious that I now wore the pants of the family – not by choice – but that is the way things stood then. It was I who had to take charge of the situation and carry the weight of responsibility for my children. Frank's mistakes had cost us, one and all, and I decided that I could not return to that state of instability. I was determined to cut off the relationship once and for all, when Frank was released from jail.

I continued to take John and James to see Frank in jail once every week, which always served to improve Frank's spirits immensely. Frank had done well for himself over the past few months, taking on responsibilities in the prison bakery and staying out of trouble.

On my weekly visits, I soon had made friends with the guards and other prison workers who treated me with cordiality and even kindness. While, for many in my position, visiting a prison might have become a source of anxiety or shame, I made the most of it. On the days that I visited, I would often take coffee to share with the guards, and together we would chat pleasantly before visiting hours began.

After Frank had been taken away and I had decided to get myself off welfare, there was no time to stand still. I needed work, and it was not long before I had picked up jobs working in the restaurant industry.

First, I worked as a prep-cook in a seafood restaurant in Hampton, New Hampshire. It was a high-pressure job, but I didn't mind. One challenge, however, did threaten to prevent me from keeping a steady job. I struggled to find someone to watch the boys for me while I was away at work. For one thing, I had little money to spare on babysitting or daycare, and the long hours I worked also made things difficult for prospective babysitters. There were no breaks, as I took on work at three jobs at the same time.

At one restaurant I met Jared, a friendly dishwasher, and we hit it off. At this point in time divorce was a certainty for me, and I decided to return to the dating world. I believed that Jared was a genuinely nice guy. What was more, he got along marvelously with John and James. Soon, Jared had moved in.

The four of us were generally happy, living together at the apartment at *The Pines*.

Yet, soon I discovered a problem. Jared was lazy. He was what one would call a *momma's boy*. He had never really needed to make it on his own because his mother supported him – financially and otherwise. Jared could never hold down a job for long and eventually, in some ways, he became dependent on me.

Jared slept all day. He would put the kids on the bus and then go back to sleep. Sometimes, he would wake up in the morning and put blankets over the windows to block out the light, and then he would sleep well into the afternoon.

I took a job working in a cafeteria at *Reilly's*, a plant that manufactured electrical fuses. I started work at 4 o'clock in the morning and ended at 2 o'clock in the afternoon. Often, I would return home after work and find Jared still sleeping, just as I had left him early that morning. Sometimes, I wondered why I would go long periods of time without receiving any phone calls. Later, I would discover that it was because Jared had unplugged the phone cords so that his sleep would not be interrupted.

I realized, in retrospect, that Jared really wasn't *all there*. He was not a real man. I believe his mother ruined him.

However, I was not overly angry with Jared. Despite his faults, he was a nice guy, and the children got along well with him. What is more, I could use him as a default babysitter. Although our relationship eventually fizzled out, he lived at *The Pine's* with me for some time.

Even when he finally moved out, the boys would often go to visit him where he had moved back in with his mother.

Jared was, for now, out of the big picture. Little did I know that a couple of years later, he would come crashing back into the scene. The result would be turmoil, which I could never have anticipated.

CHAPTER TWENTY

XENAPHOBIA

You are a thief, and you are fired!" roared the tall Irish woman, Molly Flanagan. Her already ruddy complexion had now turned to a violent shade of purple. Her rotund form shuddered angrily with each word she bellowed. Her attitude now showed, in no uncertain terms, her hatred towards me; there was nothing covert about it. She began to froth at the mouth and sweat fiercely. It seemed to me, a woman of her dimensions would always be on the verge of a heart-attack and, by the look of things, she might have had *the big one* if she hadn't calmed down soon.

"Pack your bags," Molly demanded. "After today, you are done."

I was not one to shy away from a fight, but I knew that I needed to stay calm. I needed to keep this job. The truth was that I had taken the food. I often took food; sometimes three times-a-day. But things were not as they seemed at first glance. It was I who was the victim here. I had done nothing wrong.

"Excuse me? Excuse me!" I answered boldly, "I did not steal!"

As the saying goes, *honesty is the best policy*, I had seen the terrible effects of dishonesty throughout my life. When my father had wanted me to lie to his employer, I paid the price. When Frank wanted to cut a deal with a mobster, even with the noble intention of keeping his business afloat, I had paid the price. I experienced the pain of remorse when, for a short time, I felt dishonest with myself by becoming dependent upon the government.

And now this large, red-faced Irish woman had called me a thief. Although I had lost much in my life, integrity was something I had always managed to hold on to. And now I clung to my innocence with defiance. *How dare Molly call me a thief! Where does she come off?*

The problem had begun months before, when I had taken up work at Reilly's. I worked in the cafeteria of the plant, running the kitchen, cooking, and serving the workers.

I needed to be at work by four to make the workers their coffee, which meant that I would need to be awake by three.

The hours alone would be enough to make most people miserable, but I had other problems – problems that threatened to crush my hitherto indomitable spirit.

I would step outdoors on cold, frosty mornings to get in my car. As I waited for my car's heater to slowly kick in and as I would brave slick, icy roads, I would ask myself if this was all there was. I would think, *Please, please, please don't let this be my life. I know this can't be it, I know I can do better.*

I wondered if all my troubles in life, all the turmoil I had experienced, everything I had overcome, and all my struggles would amount to this dead-end job, persecuted daily by discrimination.

Truly, difficulty was nothing new to me. *What was one more disappointment? Would I really settle for rock bottom?*

I had experienced difficulty, but I had also experienced comfort and stability. Once, I had fur coats, Rolex watches and a comfortable place to live. Once, I had a husband to help take the pressures of life and to bear the responsibilities of parenthood.

But now, I had none of that. What had happened, to bring me to this point? I was a German citizen, living in America, and I was not experiencing the *American Dream* either. The bills stacked up easily, making quitting this job a risk I could not afford to take.

Might apathy soon begin to creep in? I thought. *Was now the time, after all I had gone through, to pull up stakes and move back to Germany? Were my sisters and mother right? Was it true that I was not cut out to make it in America on my own merit?*

Does everything happen for a reason? Can we really make the most of our circumstances, or are there some lucky ones; then others who will simply never get by? I had told myself that this just could not be it – the final straw – and I clung resolutely to this one hope. I knew I could change my lucky stars, but how would I make it out of this predicament now? Would Molly fire me? Why was Molly so angry at me in the first place?

In short, Molly was a bigot. Day-in and day-out, she ground me down on the jobsite by belittling me and making my life miserable. She had a dislike – even a hatred – for me. She was a xenophobia, which prevented her from looking past nationality to see that I was just another person; a mother, a sister, a daughter trying to get by without bothering anyone. She seemed to have a particular dislike for Germans, and this dislike found a target in her underling, me.

I had encountered xenophobia before, and I would continue to experience it long into the future. Years later, I would find a Swastika keyed into a panel of my car. Once, when I had worked at the donut shop, an elderly, probably dementia-ridden, man had demanded that I tell him why the Germans had started "The War." I had not taken it personally then, but now I found myself unable to escape this kind of discrimination.

It was ironic that Molly hated Germans, because the owner of the manufacturing company was a German himself. Shmidt was his name. Ironic too, that this thoroughly Irish woman would put me under the same discrimination that so many Irish men and women had suffered earlier in American history. George Santayana is often quoted in his book, *Reason in Common Sense*: "Those who cannot remember the past, are condemned to repeat it." And I repeat it here.

Molly would wear me down in a variety of different ways, but the same attitude of disdain remained almost constant.

For example, I knew the factory workers were fond of me, especially because of my specialty in home fries, which never failed to bring praise. Whenever I made home fries, Molly would send me away so that I would not receive any praise or attention. Once she thought I was out of earshot, Molly would insult me insisting that I was generally useless in the kitchen, except when it came to cooking German food.

Molly pounced on me every time there was a communication error, using it as an excuse to mock my limited knowledge of the English language. In the kitchen, the old refrigerators and other equipment hummed loudly through the day, making it difficult for anyone to be understood over the noise. Nevertheless, Molly took every opportunity to insist that, "If you want to talk to Renata, or if you want Renata to understand you, you have to speak German."

Molly put me down so often, I was brought to tears almost daily.

The factory workers would ask me if I was okay, remarking that my eyes were red. I couldn't tell them that I had been crying in the bathroom. I simply tried to keep a stiff upper lip, and carry on as normal.

Frequently, when I accomplished a task, Molly would force me to do it over again, completely arbitrarily. She would say "You don't know how to do it right, you are German, do it over again."

Molly wasn't a thoroughly wicked woman, although she did make my life difficult. She was, however, intolerably moody, and I was the one who stood to suffer at the mercy of these unpredictable moods.

Yet, Molly was not always in a bad mood. After meals, virtually every day, an excess of food would be prepared. When there were leftovers, she would often allow me to take food home.

"Take it for your kids, you need it," she would say.

The alternative was to throw out the leftovers. If anything, allowing me to take it home, rather than letting it rot, was only common sense and nothing overly generous.

On this day, Molly's mood had taken a sour turn. She was out for blood, and it looked like there would be trouble for "…that stupid German."

I had helped Jared to get a job working the second shift at Reilly's. It was my habit to fix him a plate of food from the excess of breakfast. I would put it in an out-of-the-way place. No harm done.

Molly saw me taking the food and hiding it away for Jared. Immediately, her prejudices took hold of her.

"What are you doing?" she demanded.

"Getting Jared a plate of food, like I always do," I answered, realizing that Molly was in a foul temper.

"You are stealing," Molly exclaimed. "You are finished here!"

Molly had not given me specific permission to take food that day. Therefore, it was clear to her that I had stolen it. If I had stolen something, that made me a thief. If I was a thief, Molly had full license to unleash a tirade on *this no-good German.*

Her blood began to boil, as she declared I was a thief. She vowed to report me to the owner of the company, and predicted that I would be fired by the end of the day.

Meanwhile, I had finally had quite enough. How could I have stolen something which was to be thrown out anyway? What was the difference between this time and all the other times that Molly had let me take food from work? In my mind, there *was* no difference. It was no mystery to me that Molly had long-fostered hatred towards me and that Molly might easily use this situation to get me fired if she could.

So rather than flying off the handle, I insisted that I had not stolen anything.

"Excuse me, I am not a thief," I insisted firmly.

But apart from that, I did not confront Molly's prejudices. Now was not the time to pick fights. I needed to keep this job. I didn't plan to lose my job, the bills would not pay themselves.

CHAPTER TWENTY-ONE

CLEANVERGNÜGEN

Molly demanded that I clean the entire kitchen myself, and I did not argue with her. Of course, cleaning out the kitchen was Molly's responsibility too, but I was not about to push this point. I went about my work, but inside I seethed over the overt discrimination and this woman who now arbitrarily threatened my job. This would not be the end of the matter, I vowed.

I scrubbed high and I scrubbed low. I mopped the floors until they glistened. I polished the stainless steel until my reflection shone in it like a mirror. I worked myself into a cleaning frenzy, using the process to tune out the anxiety that threatened to crush me. As I cleaned, the radio blared loudly in the background. Suddenly, to my surprise, I realized that the voice on the radio was speaking German.

It was a Volkswagen commercial. That year, Volkswagen had tried a novel approach to reach the American market. In the advertising industry, as everyone knows, unique and memorable catch-phrases are often what gets the product sold. Often, the stranger the buzzword, the better. In this case, the advertisement's tagline was the German word *Fahrvergnügen*.

It was a mouthful of a word for the English speaking world. What is a Fahrvergnügen? A medical condition of some kind?

If it were not for the prospect of being fired, while at the same time cleaning like a fiend, while at the same time listening to a commercial which only ran for a few months, I might never have come up with the idea of Cleanvergnügen. Instead of *driving enjoyment*, which is what Fahrvergnügen means, it would be *cleaning enjoyment*.

So, at this time, all I had was a name: *Cleanvergnügen*. But, I had some business cards made up and determined to make a start. I was still not sure how to proceed, but I told myself, *I am going to start with one house, and take it from there.*

This year marks my twenty-fifth year of business, a quarter-century of success. One could almost say, to coin a phrase, that the rest is history, but I had many difficulties yet to face. I had been accused of stealing and would need to handle the situation before moving on. And there was another disaster looming on the horizon; something I could never have predicted, but which threatened to tear my family apart. Soon, I would experience the shock of my life.

CHAPTER TWENTY-TWO

OVERCOMING DISCRIMINATION

The problem of 'stealing' was not about to go away. For one thing, I was not one to allow myself to be fired on the whim of a woman who, for all intents and purposes, was a racist. I had never been accused of stealing – not in Germany, and not in any of the odd jobs I had worked since moving to America. Even while I had lived with Frank, who had certainly experienced his share of scrutiny for his business practices, my integrity never came into question.

My good name, at present, was all I had and I was determined to make sure that it came through this ordeal unscathed. I stood to lose so much otherwise. Who would want to hire a thief? How would anyone ever be able to trust me again? I knew when to pick my fights and that time was now.

I knew the owner of the company, Ron Shmidt, and decided to write him a letter. Aided by a friend who helped me to compose a grammatically-correct message, I outlined the events of the debacle and pled with Ron to let me keep my job. After receiving the letter, Ron agreed to meet with me, and together we discussed the circumstances.

I told Ron how moody Molly was; that she let me take food home, and then she accused me of stealing.

"I can't believe this whole story." Ron mused, "She is so moody that she tried to get you fired when she was in one of those moods?"

Often, when Molly permitted, I borrowed a pan from the kitchen to carry the food home.

I told Ron that I couldn't have walked out of there with one of those big pans, without Molly knowing about it; that I still had one at home. I told him I would bring it to him to prove it. There was no way I could have left the premises with such a large pan without Molly observing me.

"You see," I concluded, "She told me to bring home food for the kids, but then, because of her moodiness, she flip-flopped and called it stealing."

Perhaps Ron did not understand, at first, what could have motivated Molly. However, my innocence was not the only issue on the table, there was also the matter of discrimination in the workplace. I announced that I was prepared to sue for the discrimination I had faced. I emphasized that if there was ever a case to be made and won, this was it.

At this announcement, Ron's approach changed drastically. Foreseeably, he could stand to lose money by a lawsuit, if it was the case that I truly was fired under false pretenses. From my account, this seemed increasingly more likely to be the case.

For almost three hours all told, we continued. He begged me not to sue and I told him that my main concern was that I did not want anyone to think that I had anything to do with thievery.

Ron expressed to me that he was sorry about the whole situation. Furthermore, he confided, he was worried what might happen if he were forced to fire Molly. Despite her faults, Molly was a central figure in his company's operations. Firing her would be a logistical nightmare. Fortunately, although I had been wronged, I was never a grudge-holding type. I did not have a vendetta against Molly, even if Molly had harassed me and brought me to tears. But for all this, I certainly could not continue to work with her.

"Renata," Ron stated. "You work for me, and so as far as I am concerned, you didn't steal anything."

As a solution, Ron asked me if I would compromise and take another, better job working at the cafeteria of a nearby power plant that he also managed. I gladly accepted. This solution kept me with a job and paying the bills, while at the same time removing me from an abusive situation. All told, Ron probably breathed a sigh of relief that I had not chosen to make things difficult.

But before I could begin my new job, an obstacle stood in my way.

I was obligated to undergo a full background check because, after all, it was a power plant and security was paramount.

I needed a clear record. They even called my mother and my high school in Germany. But this did not worry me. However, what did worry me was the aptitude test I was also required to take. It was a bit more involved than a basic aptitude test, and the idea brought me a great deal of anxiety. On my last day on the job at Reilly's manufacturing plant, Molly (predictably) made her last parting shot.

"You are German," she said, in characteristic fashion, "you will never pass the test."

"Excuse me," I said, with justifiable indignation. "Why might that be?"

"You can't read or write English," Molly retorted.

"There, you might be a little bit right," I replied. "But Ron wants me to get the job, and if I have any problems, I'm sure that the test administrators will help me out."

"My daughter just tried to get a job at that power plant, and she had a hard time." Molly replied, doubtfully. "You won't understand half of the questions."

"Molly," I replied, indifferent to this attempt to undermine my confidence, "We will have to wait and see. How do you know what I can and cannot understand? Leave this to me."

At this time, it is true, I still struggled to read and write in English. Consequently, understanding the questions was the hardest part for me. I needed to be sure that I was reading the questions properly before answering, or I might suffer from silly mistakes. Were the test in German, no doubt it would be a breeze. But that was not an option. Going into the test, I knew that I would need iron-clad concentration to pass. But although the pressure was high, I was fortunate in that there was no time limit, and I could take my time to understand each question.

As I sat down to take the test, I was horrified to learn that there were almost five-hundred multiple choice questions. There were simple questions, trick questions, ridiculous questions, and the repetitive questions that had three different ways to trip up the test-taker. What was your mother's maiden name, what was your father's first name, what is your race? Are you white, are you black? it asked, for example.

Five other prospective employees took the test with me. Everyone, I noticed, finished the test in under an hour, apparently with great ease and confidence. The first hour passed slowly, but I was still a long way from finishing. The other participants were not allowed to move along until the entire group had completed the test. Soon, two hours had passed, and the others were growing impatient about the wait. Still, I kept blazing on, question by question. Soon they began to grumble and pressure me to finish.

"I'm on my fourth cup of coffee, for goodness sakes," one said. "What is taking you so long?"

But I did not let the pressure get to me, as I continued on at my own pace. After three hours, my determination paid off and I proudly handed in my test to the administrator. Soon, I was pleased to learn that I had passed the test.

Molly was less than excited, but she could not help but acknowledge my achievement. "I never expected it, especially because you are German and couldn't understand English," she later admitted, begrudgingly.

Sadly, Molly had forgotten that America is a country of immigrants; a place where it is supposed to accept that anyone can make it from nothing, if they set their sights high and are willing to put in the work. I had proved Molly wrong. Honestly, I couldn't care less for other's opinions of my limitations. I had been proving the naysayers wrong my whole life, and I was not about to stop now. I am continually fond of saying, "The sky's the limit!"

There are always people trying to tell you what you should do and what you can and can't do. They put you down because they can't do it themselves and are merely jealous of your success. But they won't do the work. So why should I care what they say?

CHAPTER TWENTY-THREE

A SHOCKING DISCOVERY

I was making strides with Cleanvergnügen. I was finally beginning to understand why America is called *the land of opportunity.*

I told myself, *I have a good business name, I am going to find myself one house to clean, and I'll see what happens.* One house led to another. A neighbor, a friend, or a relative would need cleaning and, if I did a good job, the word would spread and I would get a recommendation.

One of my first big contracts came through from a local country club located in a scenic coastline area of New Hampshire

I had to be there at five o'clock in the morning, seven days a week. I cleaned everything, even golf shoes.

But I didn't care, I was getting in while the getting was good.

How did I have the business acumen to build a strong operation, with a wide clientele base? My business success all stemmed from what is perhaps the most basic, but perhaps also the most often overlooked, ingredient for success: Honesty. Honest work and honest words.

I staunchly believe that honesty and dependability are the most important things in business. Part of this includes being yourself. I always encourage people to not put up a front and never try to fake it.

I always try to listen to my clients and take their advice, whenever possible. I don't have *the customer is always right* attitude. Sometimes, the customer is wrong and if you are honest with them about it, they will usually appreciate it. Sometimes they are right, and sometimes I am right. If I know I am right, I will tell them so.

Making sure that a client is happy is the goal. But you can't always make everyone happy, so I have found that it is also important to stay away from negative people. It can, and usually does, drag everything down.

Every job is different; the people are different, the details are different. It is important to have good people skills. There have been many times when I felt like exploding, but I kept my cool and it always served me well. Don't burn bridges with anyone, if you can help it.

My company grew progressively over the next couple of years, not in fits and starts. The important thing was, I believed, that hard work and honesty would pay off. I never tried to cut corners to make it big fast. Living with Frank, I had seen the terrible effect that sort of approach can bring.

Before long, I began running advertisements in the local newspaper. Business was thriving and I was determined to make the most of it, almost working around the clock.

I can handle it, for now, I thought. *When I am older, I will need something to fall back on.*

For now, life seemed stable for me and my sons. But, once again, disaster was about to strike.

I was reading the paper after work at eleven o'clock at night, and I noticed a headline concerning a recent arrest of a local man. The charge was for child pornography. After a brief glance over the article, I did a double-take. There, on the page before me, was the face of none other than Jared, my one-time boyfriend.

I was simultaneously angered and petrified. It was the man I had dated for quite some time. Was this the kind of person he really was all along? This was the man with whom I had entrusted my children, day after day, over the past couple of years. Was he really this disturbed all along? First I experience nausea, then the righteous anger of a mother bear came bursting out of me.

I called his mother and said, "If I find that Jared tried anything on either of my boys, he will be in a world of hurt!"

She said, "Oh, please don't do anything, he has gone through so much trouble already!"

"He has gone through so much trouble?" I repeated, aghast.

Was this woman joking? Was she really more worried about adding discomfort to her son, which he amply deserved for his wicked deeds, than she cared for the possible trauma two young children might have undergone at the hands of a pedophile?

"Let me tell you," I replied, with emphasis, "If I find out he even so much as touched them, or tried anything at all, then he will be in trouble." With that I hung up the phone.

The next day, after a brief investigation, I was relieved to find that neither of my sons had undergone any abuse. However, as might be imagined, the feeling of disgust and horror has lingered with me to this day.

Meanwhile, Frank had been out of jail for quite a while. As he learned of the arrest in the news, he experienced his own attack of fear as well. What had happened to his sons while he was in jail, helpless to aid them?

"When I got out of jail, this was the guy I would see sitting with my kids on the steps outside their house. I wanted to find him and wring his neck! But because I was under probation, I knew I would be in big trouble if I didn't keep my cool," Frank would later say.

It was the shock of my life. Any time things floated along smoothly, it seemed that rough waters were looming just ahead. Tragedy was bound to strike. I reflected on the horrors of what might have been, and resolved never to let anything come between me and my children ever again. Little did I know that another obstacle was just around the corner and it would threaten to tear my family apart – yet again.

CHAPTER TWENTY-FOUR

JAMES

I had no family around and no one to help me support my children. Everything rested on me and, even at a young age, my children recognized this. I celebrated both Father's Day and Mother's Day. When Father's Day came around, my kids would say, "Happy Father's Day, Mom." I would chuckle wryly at this.

I tried to pay as much attention to my sons as I could. I gave them lots of presents and tried to do everything I could to keep up with them. I know, though, that they still had a very hard time. They saw that other parents were attending every sporting event and had predictable schedules. I tried to be there as much as I could, of course, but I could never catch a break from working. I think that, when they were younger, they couldn't understand why I was absent so often. I tried my hardest for the kids, I don't think there was much else I could have done. I believe that now that they are older, they know that I tried my best. But it was tough on them, there is no denying. No one else was bringing home the bacon.

I believe that it's important for children to have a father around. I don't know if my sons would be better off now if Frank had been around, but it would have taken some pressure off me, and the kids would have had more attention from their parents.

The main reason I stayed in America was for my children. I could have moved us all back to Germany where life might have been easier in some ways, but I wanted for them to have the best, and that meant staying in America. I believed that it would be best for them to be near Frank too, if possible.

Yet my boys were stood up by their father throughout their childhood. He told them that he was forced to pick between them and the woman in his life, and he picked the woman. Even when he lived in the area before he moved to Florida, he would tell them that he was going to pick them up and then would skip out on them. I believe that it must have affected them terribly.

They asked, "Why didn't he come? He said he would."

Soon, it began to make me look bad too, because I would tell them that their father was coming and when he never showed up, it made me look like a liar.

It is hard to say exactly why, but I had trouble with James from a young age. James suffered from a terrible, uncontrollable temper, which only grew worse as he grew older.

I can't explain why James and John ended up differently. I treated both my sons the same. But James' problems began very early on, even when he was in kindergarten. I sent him to a private parochial school and, even at that young age, his teachers had trouble with him. He was difficult to manage. Maybe, at first, he wasn't necessarily a troublemaker but he always attracted attention in a negative way. He interrupted, he didn't want to follow directions and he generally made things difficult on the nuns.

He would have 'episodes'. Sometimes he would sit there like the nicest kid, but then something would set him off and he would become so angry, as if he was going to kill the world.

From a young age James was manipulative. In school, he would tell his teachers, "I am going to kill you." Or, at recess, he would be out on the playground and he would tell his classmates something to the same effect. Whenever he pulled that sort of thing, the school policeman would then come and take him to the nurse's office and he would have the day off from school – which is, of course, just what he wanted.

I had a conference with some of the people at James' school, and told them what was happening. I told them that we needed to turn this around. I knew exactly what he was doing. He just didn't want to be in school. He had figured it out at age eleven that he could get off that way. It happened many, many times.

I told them that for this behavior to stop, they needed to stop pulling him out of class and that we needed to call his bluff.

Thankfully, the teachers took this into consideration. Whenever James would threaten them, a teacher would laugh it off and say, "You don't mean that James, I know that you like me, you don't really want to kill me."

The teachers tried this approach a couple of times, and they were never threatened again from that time forward. But James' problems, sadly, were only just beginning.

Many times, he had awful tantrums and would begin to kick and punch the walls. At these times, the police would take him to the hospital. They were concerned for his mental health and his own safety, so he ended up at the emergency room and was evaluated by Seacoast Mental Health.

Often, he tried to get people in trouble. Once, he had an episode and was taken to the hospital again. On this occasion, however, he was taken to a different hospital over an hour away. John and I went to see him. But, because he had just had a violent outburst, our visitation was supervised. We stayed for a while, and during that time he had another tantrum – this time he threw a chair.

"We are going home, James," I told him. Even though we had driven an hour out to see him, I was not going to tolerate that kind of behavior.

We left him at the hospital where he was to stay overnight, and returned home. There, a shocking twist awaited me.

When we arrived, there was a message on the answering machine. The hospital had called while we were on the road and they requested that I return their call immediately.

James had reported that I had hit him.

"Child abuse?" I responded, dumbfounded.

I could not believe my ears after my own experiences with my father.

"Wait a minute," I recalled after a moment's reflection. "Wasn't the visitation supervised? And don't you have cameras in that room?"

"Yes, we do," they replied.

"Well," I suggested, "Please do me a favor, and go take a look at the footage. I didn't touch him."

As might be assumed, I was justifiably angry that they had not checked the security tape before calling. The woman on the line agreed to call me back, and only ten short minutes later, the phone rang. She admitted that I hadn't done anything, and that was the end of that.

It was a terrible situation. James quickly became vicious –I would say, even dangerous. When he had an episode, we noticed that his eyes changed as the anger came over him. He had authority issues, no matter the authority. But, especially if it was me. One year, when James was on vacation, he went down to Florida to visit Frank. After a while, Frank could not manage him and he had to send him back up to New Hampshire.

Once, he threatened to kill me when he was out of control. I had to call the police, because I was legitimately scared. The police arrived, and were going to take him with them, but he didn't want to go and he ran into the kitchen and grabbed an apple peeler. The policeman thought it was a knife and drew his gun. He might have shot James.

"James, you are very lucky to be alive," the policeman said, as he took James away.

I didn't know what to do with myself, I was so upset. We went to court, and there I saw the most terrible thing I have ever seen. I saw my little son, dressed in an orange jumpsuit with handcuffed feet and legs, sitting there as if he was one of the killers that you see on television. He was only twelve. To me, it was the most revolting picture. I didn't know what to do.

I enlisted the help of Seacoast Mental Health. We arranged a placement for school, including a home he could stay in during the school week, and arranged for him to be home on the weekends. Everything was arranged, but then the court made a decision that I now believe was the worst thing they could have done. The court decided to send James away to live with Frank in Florida.

I asked some people from Seacoast Mental Health and a couple of teachers to come and support me at court. They agreed to speak to the judge, if they were allowed, to advise him that it would be a bad decision to send James to Florida.

James' lawyer asked James, "Do you feel uncomfortable that all these people are here?"

"My mom can stay in the room, but I want everyone else to get out," James replied, seizing the opportunity to make trouble.

He smiled at me throughout the proceedings, as if to say, *see mom, you can't do anything about me now; see mom, now I am paying you back.* It was heart destroying.

Everyone who was there for him was sent out. However, I realize now that it wasn't James' fault. Why were they asking a child what was best for his wellbeing? He's only a kid, a troubled child. Seacoast Mental Health had a placement already set up. The court could have taken advantage of that, but instead they chose to tear him away from his home and all the people who were working so hard to help him. That is why, I believe, the court is responsible. James fell through the cracks. There was a time when something could have been done. But it seems to me, they just wanted him out of their hands.

It was a big mess. I had been there for the kids since they were born, but now Frank was interfering by offering to take James. The court was completely against me. They didn't even take my wishes into consideration. I was sitting in the courtroom and no one asked me a single question.

Seacoast Mental Health could not believe the court's decision. After everything we had worked so hard for, they had decided to send James to Frank. Moving James to Florida didn't improve anything. He pulled the same things with Frank that he had done with me. I felt terrible about it, but what could I do? I was in over my head when the court made the decision to send him to Frank.

After everything I had done for my son, it just wasn't good enough. The court didn't trust me; they thought that they knew best. Sometimes the justice system ends up working out, sometimes it doesn't.

When our case was over, I approached James' lawyer.

"You are making a big mistake," I told him. "You are just doing this to get James out of your hair."

"But Renata," he said, "he will be out of your hair, too!"

"Excuse me?" I replied aghast, "You are talking about my son!" I was disgusted. "You are making a big mistake, sending him away."

"Why is that?" he asked

"You have children too, don't you?" I knew that he did. "Can't you see how bad this is?"

"Yes, but Frank is his biological father. Don't you think he has a right to be with his father?" he replied.

"No, I don't," I replied. "His father has never played a role in James' life."

The court could have put him in placement at school, where he would have lived until he was an adult. It would have helped him a lot. Everything was all set up, we just needed the judge's go-ahead. Instead, the court decided to send him to his father. Even though we had stacks of documentation to show that this was not a good idea – you don't have to be a doctor to figure it out. Seacoast Mental Health had files and files on him. They decided, however, to send him to Florida. That didn't solve anything, it just put the problem in a different state. I believe that the court's decision was the catalyst for all of the problems he has now.

Today, he is a ticking time bomb. He needs help, but not any kind of help that I can give him. I believe that he needs to be in the mental health system, in an assisted living arrangement where people can check in on him. He doesn't listen to me.

I try to help him, but he has issues that have never been resolved. I tell him that if he doesn't want to change, he won't. If he doesn't want to make things better for himself, no one else will do it for him.

The court should not have let a person in that condition go. Now, no one is looking after him since he is old enough to be on his own. There is nothing anyone can tell him. I check in on him and he doesn't listen to me. He thinks that he can handle everything because he is an adult now, but that is not the case.

He should not be alone, he should be living in a group home or something to help him. For one thing, he doesn't have the street smarts to really take care of himself and his living conditions are terrible. I have invited him to live with me many times. But he has admitted and, if I am honest, I must admit myself that we would have big issues. I have rules and he wouldn't be able to live any way he wants to in my house. I tried. I tried so hard. But now there is nothing I can do. There was nothing I could do once the court stepped in. It's so very, very sad. He doesn't have the ability to take care of himself.

James found out that, if one stays at the homeless shelter for a given amount of time, the state will pay for housing. So, the state pays for his housing. Now he has no ambition to get out on his own and try to improve himself. He is stuck and has no desire to get anything better than a part-time job.

I feel terrible for the way things have turned out and I constantly ask myself what I could have done differently.

When I was a child, I suffered because nobody stepped in to halt my father's abuse. Now, as a mother, I am experiencing the other end of the spectrum: having my son taken away from me.

As with most of the terrible blows I have received throughout my life, my solution is to shrug off the negativity and hope and look forward to my son one day becoming a healthier and happier person.

CHAPTER TWENTY-FIVE

A GREEN CARD NO MORE

At first, I hesitated to obtain American citizenship. To take advantage of Frank's citizenship in order to expedite the process, was the farthest thing from my mind when I first came to America. For one thing, when I arrived I was not sure how long I would stay. Furthermore, I did not want to be known as someone who married into American citizenship, as was so common in Germany at the time. I had come to America not because I was particularly unhappy with Germany, but for the preservation of my family.

The problem was that now I had divorce Frank, I found myself surrounded by limitations that came with my position living in the United States as a foreigner. I had stayed in America through thick and thin, and now that I was beginning to hold a true stake in the United States I knew that citizenship was a necessity. True, I had a green card but I still found myself limited in many ways, and now I had no pathway to citizenship through Frank.

At one point, I wanted to get a position working at the nearby Portsmouth Naval Shipyard. It would have been a good job cleaning offices there, but I was not allowed on base because I was not an American citizen. Working and voting were my top reasons for seeking American citizenship.

Throughout my 25-year career, I cleaned the offices of some of New Hampshire's United States Senators and a couple of Representatives as well. Over the years, I developed a friendly relationship with many of the people who worked in these offices. One woman in particular, Ingrid, consistently encouraged me to get my citizenship.

I knew I would have to take the test and I began studying. But everyone told me that it would be a piece of cake; that it wouldn't be that hard. So I didn't worry. I went to take the take the test and found that it wasn't as easy as I had thought it would be.

The man who gave the verbal part of the test asked me, "Who is Martin Luther King Junior?"

I had never really studied American History. I had some vague ideas, but I wasn't too sure of the right way to answer, so I replied, "He is the guy who said, 'I had a dream'."

"That's not the answer I am looking for," the test administrator replied.

"What answer are you looking for?" I asked.

"You should have mentioned the Civil Rights Movement. Sorry, you are going to have to take the test again in three months."

I was kicking myself because I thought it would be so easy. So I said to myself, *you really need to buckle down and study hard now.*

One day I saw a friend at the bank. She knew that I had taken the test and she asked me how it had gone. I told her that I had flunked it, that it wasn't that easy. I was friends with a few people at the bank, so I asked them there, on the spot, a few of the questions which were on the test. One woman didn't even know how many stars there were on the flag and she was an American citizen.

Over the next three months, I studied to the point of exhaustion. Along the way, I learned how difficult the test really was. I was determined to learn everything that could be asked from A-to-Z. Some days, my son John helped me to study after work. He would ask me question after question until my brain fried.

Over the course of my study I learned how important American history is, and how important it is for the youth of today to learn it. Although I already had a cultural identity as a German, I came to learn the importance of the American heritage.

My hard work studying paid off, and I passed the test with flying colors the second time around. I knew that I had prepared when I was able to answer what was perhaps the most obscure question of the test: Who wrote the *Star Spangled Banner*, and when was it written?

Francis Scott Key, 1814.

America is sometimes called a country of immigrants, and now I was officially added to the list. Naturally, I had much invested in the United States long before I had made the final decision to go for my citizenship. At that time, I had two sons who were born in America, I paid taxes, and I owned a home and a business of some fifteen years.

Perhaps knowing who the twenty-first President was does not have that much of an impact on what kind of citizen a new immigrant will become. However, there are certainly relevant things which everyone ought to know when they try to become naturalized citizens. I believe that the main thing is that it should be easy for people who already have a stake in America to obtain citizenship.

Let it be said, however, that I am not in favor of amnesty for illegal immigrants. I believe that everyone should follow the laws and not immigrate illegally in the first place, if they can help it. As an immigrant who worked her way up from nothing, I am not in favor of any freebies or rule-bending. I never looked for any freebies either, except for my short stint on food stamps.

The best advice I could give to immigrants is not to depend upon the government. Contribute. Try to make it by yourself. Don't be a burden. Even if immigrants are coming to America with nothing but the shirts on their backs as I did, I hope that they will bring the right attitude with them. They need to want to succeed, that is what this country needs.

It begins with learning English, I strongly believe. I have known some immigrants who have lived in the U.S. for ten, even fifteen years, and can't speak any English. I think that it is essential all Americans should learn English, just so everyone can be on the same page. Years ago, I never thought I would be able to speak English as well as I do today. It was hard, but it had to happen.

Immigrants should also work hard at learning the laws of the land. Through my experience, I have realized that you should never assume that the laws are the same everywhere. They might be different in the U.S. than where one is migrating from, in big or little ways. For example, I had an incident when I first came to America that almost ended in disaster because I was not paying attention to rules which seemed to me to be unimportant at the time.

When I lived in Germany I got my driver's license, which was (at least at that time) a much more complicated process than getting a driver's license in the United States. For one thing, the process for getting a license is much more expensive. I believe it was in the region of three thousand dollars. Part of the reason why is because their driver's education is very extensive.

When I came to America, I passed the driving test and got my license with no trouble. The rules in America are mostly the same as Germany. We drive on the same side of the road but in Germany, turning right on a red light is not allowed.

I passed the test, but I didn't understand what a lot of the signs meant. One thing that I had no experience with, at the time, was school buses. In Germany, we didn't have them. When we lived in Hampton, New Hampshire, Frank worked as a used car salesman so we had a car. One day, I was driving on my way home from work and a school bus had stopped in the middle of the road. Cars had stopped on either side of the road too. I did not know what was going on.

Why is everyone just sitting there? I thought. *Just drive around it!* So, I stepped on the gas and zipped up to the front of the line, speeding past the bus.

Stupid Americans! I thought at the time.

I got home, and said to Frank, "You should have seen these stupid people. Like sheep. All stopped in the middle of the road. Americans can't drive, they didn't have the common sense to drive around a bus!"

"Was it a yellow bus, with red signs?" he asked.

I didn't know what the color of the bus had to do with it, but when he explained it to me I was horrified. I felt my whole face turn white. To think that I might have run over a whole group of children!

At first, I thought that they should have given me a book of driving rules. But now I realize that the lesson of the story is that it is important, as an immigrant, to go out of one's way to learn the ins and outs of the American way of doing things.

America is what you make of it. That is what I have learned.

CHAPTER TWENTY-SIX

UNDER ARREST

Please step out of the vehicle, and place your hands on the hood of the car. You are under arrest." the police officer said gruffly.

I saw my livelihood flashing before my eyes. What would this arrest mean? Could it have the power to unravel my life's work, my integrity? How could I escape from the situation I now found myself in?

It was a clear fall day on November 7, 2000. It was unseasonably warm; few would have complained. It was also windy. Short gusts of wind blew the last straggling leaves from the bare treetops. They were the winds of change, not only for the weather, but also for the nation. November 7th was the day of the 2000 presidential election.

Everywhere, Americans went about their business, ignorant of the imminent weeks of coming turmoil that would surround the voting process. I, for one, was only too happy to have participated at the ballot box. I was a fresh-out-of-the-box, newly-naturalized American citizen. And I was proud of it. As I turned in my ballot and exited the poll, I could not have guessed that I was about to experience my own measure of chaos.

President Calvin Coolidge once stated, "The chief business of the American people is business." I had sought American citizenship primarily for two reasons: to vote and to work. Today, I would proudly perform both.

My business revolves around a system of trust. In offices and houses, it need hardly be said, valuables are to be found. At times, I operate alone, in the midst of opulence or commercially-valuable items and, not to forget, sentimentally priceless belongings. Someone with less scruples and lighter fingers might be tempted to 'liberate' loose valuables, if they ever found a chance. Certainly, chances have arisen where

I could have chosen to take advantage of my situation. But that is not the kind of person I am. When I'm in a house, I won't touch a penny. Trust is everything, and I treat other's homes as if they were my own. But even if I had decided to change my approach, it would have taken a lot to appear untrustworthy. My clients operate under the assumption that the person they are letting into their house will not let them down. It stands to reason that if they found their cleaning woman had been arrested, even if they were unsure of the circumstances, an arrest alone might destroy this crucial sense of trust and make a business relationship impossible.

One day, this is exactly how I found myself.

While Cleanvergnügen was still getting off the ground, I would fill in the gaps in my schedule by working in a program which helped to take care of handicapped people.

That week, I was helping to take care of a man who, a few years before, had been handicapped by a stroke that prevented him from living by himself. Fred had moved in with his mother, Marge. Marge watched him every day. She never had a break, so she decided to take a well-deserved vacation. Marge applied for the handicapped assistance program and they, in turn, had recommended me. I had an interview to fill the position, she liked me, and so I got the job. Everything went smoothly at first.

I heard that *Best Buy* was having a sale on computers that same week, and I wanted to buy one. The local store had sold out of a particular model and the next closest place I could find that model, at the time, was in Concord, New Hampshire, a forty-five minute drive from Portsmouth.

I was watching Fred, however, so I could not take off an hour and-a-half to buy the computer. Fortunately, Fred's brother Charles had come to visit for a while and he told me, "Don't worry about it, I can watch my Fred for a couple of hours. You go ahead and drive to Concord."

I took John with me, got in the car, and took off to Concord. I bought the computer with no problem. I was running a little late on my way back and I didn't want to take advantage of Charles. Since I was trying to get there on time, I was speeding. I admit it.

I had sped through a sleepy coastal town which, for the purpose of this story, shall remain nameless.

Of course, the one time I happened to be speeding, the police are there to catch me at it. I was pulled over and the officer went through the typical drill, "License and Registration please," etc.

I gave him the paperwork. Now I was nervous, because I knew that Charles would need to leave and I didn't want to leave Fred alone by himself, even for a while. Not that there was necessarily any danger, but it would be unprofessional, of course. It would also be a breach of the contract I had signed with Marge. I sat there waiting patiently, as the policeman seemed to take his good, sweet time.

After a few minutes, which seemed like hours, the policeman returned with my papers. I already knew that he did not seem like the let-you-off-with-a-warning type of guy, so I expected to receive a ticket; probably the maximum fine he could make it. But what happened next shocked me terribly.

The police officer told me to get out of the car and advised me that I was under arrest. I was in shock, naturally. I cooperated with him but I asked him why I was under arrest. I knew I had been speeding, but I felt I had done nothing that warranted being under arrest. I wasn't even in a school or construction zone.

"Why am I under arrest?" I asked.

Meanwhile, John, who was sitting in the front seat, was pleading my case.

"You are making a big mistake, officer," he said. "My mother has never done a bad thing in her life, she has never been ticketed. She doesn't have anything on her record. She's on the straight and narrow, I'm telling you. She doesn't even have a credit card!"

"You are under arrest for driving under a suspended license," the officer directed towards me.

This only made John all the more incredulous.

"My mother always pays her bills," he said. "She would know better than to drive under a suspended license. You are making a big mistake."

I reassured the officer that there must be some kind of mistake. "My license is good, I guarantee it." I was so scared.

"I ran you through the computer. Renata Plitzko of Portsmouth, New Hampshire. That's you all right!"

Despite everything, I was cooperative. I stepped out of the car and put my hands behind my back. He handcuffed me behind my back, and asked me to sit in the back seat of the cruiser.

"How can I sit with my hands behind my back in this awkward position?" I asked.

I had been stopped, as it happened, on one of the busiest street corners, on one of the major thoroughfares of the town. As the officer handcuffed me, I could not help but feel shamed by the many passersby who slowed to watch the proceedings.

"This is a big mistake," was all I could manage to say.

I was no expert in the American legal system, but I knew that when an arrest is made, the arresting officer is supposed to read the suspect their rights. I realized that the officer had not read me *The Miranda Act*, and I made a note of it.

Traffic crawled by, slowed by curious drivers looking to see what sort of hoodlum was being arrested. Much to my dismay, I recognized not one, not two, but three of my clients; even making eye contact with them. I began to think that this public arrest might affect more than my driving record.

The car had to be towed away. John was driving age at the time, but he had just had his license suspended. He used to modify his car to make it seem sportier, doing things like making the exhaust too loud. Some of those things weren't legal in the state of New Hampshire and after getting pulled over one too many times, his license had been taken away for a while.

Another officer arrived and checked through the car for contraband, before allowing the tow-truck operator to hook the car and take it away. He noticed the stack of keys that I had. Working in the cleaning business, I had many duplicate house and office keys.

I realized that if the word got out that I had been arrested, my livelihood might be destroyed. Here was this big stack of keys people had entrusted to me that gained access to their homes. Sometimes, as I went about my business cleaning, I might be alone in a multi-million dollar house. If the word got out that I had been arrested, my clients might begin to think that I could not be trusted, regardless of the validity of the charges or any pending conviction.

On top of everything, I was worried about my current job. I had no way, now, of calling Charles. He would need to leave, and I was responsible for Fred if anything should happen to him while he was left alone. I began to think of how I, unintentionally, had betrayed Marge's trust. If Marge complained, I would likely be prevented from doing any future work in the Assisted Living industry in the future.

The car was towed away and 'disconsolate me' was also taken away. The police officer headed downtown towards the police station, and soon pulled into the parking lot.

As the arresting officer exited the vehicle, he was met by an older and more distinguished-looking policeman, evidently his superior. After a couple of seconds talking, the older officer began to raise his voice and his face became flushed with anger.

I realized that, by coincidence, we had arrived at the station simultaneously with the Chief of Police.

As the Chief continued to berate his subordinate, I was taken out of the car.

"Why would you handcuff her? What are you doing?" the Chief exclaimed, angrily.

I realized that I was finally getting the upper hand in this ridiculous proceeding. "I tried to explain to this officer," I said to the Chief, "that he was making a mistake. But what did he say? He said, *Ma'am don't talk.*"

"Get those handcuffs off of her," he demanded, fuming.

By listening to their conversation, I discovered that this was not the first time this sort of thing had happened. Apparently, the arresting officer had made false arrests before.

As the handcuffs were removed, I seized the moment to point out to the Chief that my wrists had been chafed by the inordinately tight cuffs.

"I have taught my two children," I told the Police Chief, "that whatever the police do is right and trustworthy. What will they think now? What will I tell them? Thank goodness I already did my voting. Is this the sort of thing that is supposed to happen in America? He never even read me my rights!"

"What can I do for you to amend the situation," the Chief replied uneasily. "We know we were in the wrong."

"How can I explain to my clients what happened? Do you know the implications of this false arrest for my business? Three of my clients saw me handcuffed on the side of the road. What can I tell them?"

Realizing that my civil rights had been infringed upon, the Police Chief attempted to do some damage control on the spot.

"I will write you up an official, signed letter explaining the circumstances of your false arrest and demonstrating your innocence. I will have it ready for you tomorrow. You can make copies and show them to anyone you wish."

Everyone who heard about the ordeal told me, "Sue them. Sue them!" I was, of course, primarily worried about the impact on my business. I am not the kind of person to go on the attack. The police had guidelines in place for the situation that had just occurred. I signed an agreement which stated that I would not sue them in the future, and they settled with me for four thousand dollars.

Isn't that a story and a half?

EPILOGUE

I had escaped turbulence on a plane throughout most of my life so far. But was it luck that pulled me through? Was it Divine providence? Does everything happen for a reason? Can one make their own luck and can attitude make all the difference?

I realize that I have had a harder life than some and, in many ways, an easier life than others. Through difficulties and tragedies, I have made it farther than I ever thought possible. I could have laid down and quit at any time. Instead, I survived pandemonium across three countries by stepping out and taking a chance on myself. Overcoming is a choice that a person can only make for themselves.

I hope that people will read this book and say to themselves, *Look how far she made it! I can improve my situation as well.* Take responsibility for yourself. No one else can.

Now, in our present economic depression, my words surely ring truer than ever.

I have been self-employed for twenty years but, if I had to, I would go and work at Dunkin' Donuts right now. You need to start somewhere. If you don't have a job, don't wait for the best possible job. It's better to always be working and pushing ahead. Never stop moving forwards.

I believe a person should always try to be self-sufficient and independent, as much as is possible.

I believe that everyone should have rules that they live by. When I was on food stamps, I was breaking my own rules of life. It made me feel ashamed. I could still be on welfare now, instead of where I am today. Don't be dependent on the government or other people. Keep a low profile, live within your means, and keep your nose to the grindstone. That is the advice I would give to young people.

Even if people put you down, don't worry about it. Attitude is what gets one ahead in life. Luck and circumstances play a role, but you have to be ready to step up. This is especially true in business.

'Class' is simply an attitude by my way of thinking.

If one has a disability or is ill, of course, that is a different thing. But I believe that America is still a place where anyone can make it. When you are just starting out, it's difficult to believe that you can afford the high cost-of-living. Some might look to the government for answers. But I say that you can get anything and everything in America, if you work for it.

You can make it happen, if you have the strength to believe in yourself.

Cleanvergnügen *good time cleaning* book is coming out soon.